Lero Six

I0541216

by

John Hash

ISBN 978-0-9831685-3-9

Other books by John Hash:

Honey Branches: The Meade Estate

Starkeeper

Lero's Mission

Go Get Nadja

Flight to Oblivion

Falcon Strike

Module 18

The characters and events in this book are fictitious. Any resemblance of any character or event to actual events or persons is unintended and coincidental.

The cover photo is a United States Navy photo, used here with gratitude.

This book is dedicated to the patriots who have given their lives to buy the precious freedoms we enjoy today.

Lero Six

Introduction

Since you arrived after things got under way, you should have an orientation so that you can participate like an old hand.

First of all, Lero is a nom de guerre. He chose that name when he was first engaged to help refurbish a British cold war strategic bomber, an Avro Vulcan, for a long distance covert mission. He proved so valuable that Jefe decided to hire him along with three other pilots to fly the plane on the mission. Lero's name is the last syllable of "pistolero." He chose that name because one of his favorite hobbies is building and shooting target pistols. Lero is a retired airline pilot, and a widower. He met Jefe and Jean during his first mission. Jean was an avionics technician who did contract work for Jefe and earned her place in the unit because of her ability to build and sometimes invent the technical electronics gear that the unit needed for its clandestine operations. Jean was married briefly in her early twenties, but is divorced and lives adjacent to Davis Monthan Air Base in Tucson. She and Lero met at a Wednesday bible study group at her church. After a couple of meetings, she invited him to dinner. They have lived together for about eighteen months now and are completely devoted to each other.

Jefe was the head of Group 47, which the members usually refer to as the "Unit." The headquarters of the unit is on the air base in a Quonset hut which was erected in the build up to World War II, but has survived the heat and sunlight of the western desert. It is up-fitted now with air conditioning and all the comforts and amenities of a modern office building, even though its exterior is pretty much as it was years ago.

Jefe is sixty four and has recently begun his retirement. President Thompson, to whom the Unit reports directly, asked Lero to take over the Unit when Jefe began his retirement.

Jefe lives with Alita, whom he has known since high school. Alita is married to George, who is in a nursing home in Tennessee after suffering a debilitating stroke several years ago. Alita's children know Jefe as a long-time family friend, but they do not know that Jefe and Alita live together. From time to time, Alita must travel to Tennessee to see to George's care and to visit with their daughters, who live about a hundred miles from the nursing home, in different cities.

Jefe and Alita alternate between their home in Tucson and his villa on Keros in the Greek Isles.

You can catch up with the group by reading "Lero's Mission," "Go Get Nadja," "Flight to Oblivion," "Falcon Strike," and "Module 18." Welcome to the unit.

Chapter 1

Lero was examining a satellite photo of an area of new, but cleverly concealed, construction at Parchin when Velma buzzed him on the intercom.

"Can you pick up a package that is being delivered by air in about an hour?" she asked.

"Sure. Where will the package be available?" he asked.

"The message says that a C-17 will drop it by at 11:45 on the south tarmac. They asked for a confirmation that you could pick it up."

"Send confirmation. Any other clue as to what it is?" he asked.

"No. Do you want me to get the motor pool to make a truck available at that time, in case it is too big to carry?"

"Yes, alert the motor pool, but tell them to be on stand-by at that time and not to come out unless either you or I call them to do so," he said.

"Will do," she said.

The fluorescent lights gave just the right about of illumination to the satellite photos. With his large magnifying glass, mounted on a goose neck, he could get as good a look at the new construction as could be had from above.

"These people are not fools," he thought. "They know we are watching. This careful concealment of the extension of Building A-12 is obvious to anyone who might be giving it his attention. By adding a row of corrugated metal sheets each day, they were deliberately expanding, but, at the same time, were concealing the advancing construction."

When he first noticed the expansion in his periodic examination of the Parchin overhead photos, he carefully measured the building with calipers, and since the satellite remained at a set altitude, he could tell each time they added a row of roofing sheets, how much area had been added. He kept a log of his periodic examinations and noted that he first noticed the expansion five months ago. By now, they had expanded building A-12 by forty percent. The roof of the building now concealed an area of ninety thousand square feet. Approximately thirty thousand square feet had been added in the last month.

Velma buzzed him away from his concentration on Building A-12.

"It is eleven thirty," she said.

"Thanks, Velma. I will be right out."

He turned off the lighted magnifying glass and stood behind his desk. The old desk had served many masters in its life at Davis Monthan Air Base. The last twelve years, though, it had not appeared on the inventory of office equipment for the base, however. It had been declared surplus and was bought at auction by a gentleman who paid cash and had a truck pick it up and the other items he bought at the auction the next day. After helping the man and his crew load up the other pieces and the desk, the Sergeant had asked the man to sign a receipt for the items. The signature and the receipt were duly filed in the report of the auction and buried in the tons of old paperwork. Jefe had signed the receipt with an assumed name that sunny day. No one recognized that he had signed the name of Douglas Corrigan to the receipt.

Lero pulled his customary light gray blanket over the maps and other papers on his desk and went out into the reception room, Velma's domain. The room was cool and the cement floor was covered with wall to wall carpet and a nice oriental rug decorated the center of the room in front of her desk. The old Quonset hut had taken to the conversion from a warehouse to an office complex with typical adaptability. The curving corrugated ceiling lent a nice uniqueness to the office.

"I don't know exactly how long this will take. Do we have any other appointments today?" he asked.

"No, nothing on the calendar," she said.

"Okay. I think I will go get a bite to eat after I pick the package up. I will be back about one."

"Fine. Do you have your cell phone in case I need to reach you?"

"Yes," he said, as he patted his pocket to reassure himself.

He strode out to his Grand Cherokee in the bleaching sunlight. It was only about a two minute drive to the south tarmac where the Transient Operations building was. Lero parked and walked in. He stopped in the lobby and checked the time. He was two minutes early. Outside, a large gray airplane was taxiing in. He immediately identified it as a C-17 and walked to the door. When it halted and cut its engines, he opened the door and stepped out onto the tarmac. The plane was a good hundred yards away and was the only transient parked there for now.

The aft cargo bay door opened and a crewman in a khaki uniform stepped out and walked hastily toward the Ops building. When he got within ten feet of Lero, he asked in a soft voice. "Are you Lero?"

Lero answered that he was Lero. The crewman turned smartly and escorted Lero to the plane. When they got to the short ladder that led to the aft cargo bay, the crewman said, "Step aboard, sir. Caution the change in light. The floor is even, though. Your package is near the front on the starboard side."

Lero stepped inside, removing his dark gray glasses as he did so. He was confident enough in his field of vision to turn to the right and stride toward the front of the cargo bay as his eyes adjusted to the dimmer light. There was an unusual bulkhead across the cargo bay about half way forward. There was a door near each side, but as he approached, the starboard door cracked open. He grasped the knob, pulled the door open and stepped inside. To the left, just out of sight of any observer in the cargo bay stood President Thompson.

"How are you, my friend," said the President as he shook hands with Lero.

"I'm fine, sir. This is a nice surprise. I am glad to see you. Is this new equipment for you, sir?"

"No, I have borrowed this from the CIA Director. I needed to leave Washington quietly. Can you stay and talk a while?"

"Yes, sir. Of course. That would be fine."

The President motioned Lero to a desk in the adjoining compartment. They went in and sat on either side of a nice walnut desk.

"Sorry to be so secretive, but I needed to see you privately." They gave each other a knowing glance.

"Is there a problem, sir?" asked Lero.

"Yes and no," said the President. "First of all, I want to tell you how grateful I am for your last mission. Choosing to fly into hostile territory in an unarmed sailplane in the middle of the night took special courage. Someday, I will demonstrate my gratitude in a more material way, but now I just want to say, 'Thanks.'"

"It was an honor to be involved, Sir. I could not have done it without Jean and Ernie, as you know."

"Yes, I know, but it was an especially ingenious plan and it took nerve and courage."

The President paused for a moment and said, "The 'no' part is troubling. We have another problem in Disneyland and I will need you and Jean and Ernie to get involved. Do you have anything cooking just now that would prevent you from devoting full time for a while to a new effort?"

"No, sir. Our schedule is so normal now that Jean is able to devote some time to her tan after work each day."

"I am so glad you and Jean found each other, Dan. I can tell by the way you talk about her that you are completely devoted to her."

"She is the best thing that ever happened to me, Sir. She is very special."

"Yes, she is. I am happy for you both."

He pulled a drawer open and got out a two inch thick jacketed folder. He put it down on the desk and pushed it over to Lero.

"This is for your eyes only and Jean's. I want you to review the information in this file and formulate a plan, including choice of personnel to carry out the mission that is outlined here. You and I will meet again in a week or so, and review and firm up our plans. I will have to contact you later to set a time and place. I want radio and telephone silence on this one. If you have questions about anything in here, write them down and we can discuss them when we meet. If you have a serious problem and want to talk before I get back in touch, call my office and leave a message that you were calling to invite me to go turkey hunting. I will get back to you."

"Sir, this seems closer to the vest than anything you have approached me about before. Is there an internal problem?"

The President smiled briefly, then said, "Your powers of intuition are impressive, Dan. Yes, we suspect we have a mole in the White House. We perceive there is no problem on your end. Tell Jean, but no one else, except Jefe and Velma."

"Will do, sir. I am sorry for the extra worry such a suspicion puts on your shoulders. We will be extra cautious."

"Good," said the President. "Now, I hate to run, but I need to be back in D.C. for a dinner meeting tonight. Tell Jean I sent my best regards and tell Jefe and Velma that I appreciate them, too."

They rose and shook hands warmly.

As they got to the door of the compartment, Lero turned and looked the President in the eyes.

"Thank you for your trust and confidence, Sir. See you soon."

"Thank you for what you do for us and our country, Dan. Take care."

Lero put his sunglasses back on as he stepped out into the glaring light. He walked directly through the Ops building and out to his car. By the time he got to the car, he could hear the engines of the great plane spool up. When he got out of his car back at his office building a couple of minutes later, he heard the C-17 power up, so he watched as it came into view over the tops of the low buildings of Davis Monthan Air Base. Soon after take-off, it turned to an easterly heading and climbed into the sun.

Chapter 2

Lero and Jean were enjoying lunch in their Grand Cherokee at the Sonic Drive in. The bright glare of the desert sun and the tinted windows and air conditioning allowed them to share some private time. He could cuddle with her on the leather seats, with one arm around her waist and she could feed him French fries as need be. As she crunched the last French fry, she asked, "Are you familiar with the term 'air gap?'"

"No, I can't say that I am. What does it mean?" asked Lero.

"It is a computer term. It means that a computer or computer system is not connected to the Internet or to any other system," she said.

"Do they have such systems for security?" asked Lero.

"You bet," she said. "That is why we needed Nadja to put viruses into the Iranian systems. We could not hack into their system from the internet. Lots of companies and state and local governments have systems with air gaps."

"Why do you bring it up?" asked Lero.

"The President specified that you not play any of the CDs that he sent on a system that is connected to the internet. We can set up a computer that will play the CDs and leave it off the internet. As a precaution, I think we should remove and destroy the hard drive of any computer we use to play those CDs. We simply cannot risk having any of the information leak out."

"Okay with me," said Lero. "I appreciate your looking over the Security Pouch that accompanied the file he gave me. He said to have you go through that first and then we could get down to business. How long do you think it will be before we can sit down and start on the file in general?"

"I can have a computer set up tomorrow. He did provide that you could read the first background file before you play the first CD, though. I will leave that pouch with you and go to the shop to get a computer set up for us. How about if you come by the shop on your way home and we can load the rig into the Cherokee?"

By now, they were nearing her shop on the east perimeter road. As he opened the door for her, he said, "I will call you as I leave the office. See you then."

She gave him a quick smooch as she stood up getting out of the car. He gave her a pat and went back to his side of the car.

In less than a minute, he was in the parking lot out front of his Quonset hut office.

Velma asked as he entered, "Was the package a big one? Did you have to get a truck?"

"No. Actually the package was small enough to carry easily. Do we have any appointments in the next couple of days?" he asked.

"No, things are quiet as far as appointments go. I can hold your calls if you need to concentrate on something," she offered.

"Velma, once again, you have read my mind. Yes, hold calls, unless you think it is important enough to interrupt me. And, without initiating contact if you can, please find out for me where Jefe is."

He went into his office with the file in his hand. He did not go to his desk, but sat at his conference table and opened the file.

Within the file was a sealed envelope. On the front was printed in large black letters. "Eyes Only." That meant that Lero could not share the file with anyone but Jean and Jefe. There was a small thermite charge in the file, too, in case it needed to be incinerated quickly. He put the file cover down and put the thermite charge on the opposite side of the table, and opened the file.

The cover letter had no heading, just a date, dated the day before.

"TO: Lero, Jean and Jefe,

We have two problems to tackle at the same time. First, since we succeeded in detonating the Iranian weapon in the mine south east of Esfahan, we have set them back considerably. They have decided to continue to develop a trigger and they do not know, we believe, that the 'accident' of last May was the act of a foreign government, but they think it was a premature detonation of their first atomic device. They are pleased that the device worked, but disappointed that the trigger malfunctioned and set off the device prematurely. In order to accelerate their development of a deliverable weapon, they have made a deal with the Russian successor to the KGB to purchase triggers for the first three devices they will manufacture.

Our sources were fortunate enough to be on the Trans Siberian Railroad at a time when they could observe three metal containers of a certain shape and size being loaded onto a freight car at Zheleznogorsk in the middle of the night. As you know, Zheleznogorsk was a secret city under the Soviets, in the province of Krasnoyarsk Krai. Only when Boris Yeltsin was elected did they finally put it on their maps. There are about eighty thousand persons who work in Zheleznogorsk now, down from ninety or so thousand in twenty ten. We think this is where the primary factory is located to manufacture triggering devices for the assorted Russian nuclear weapons. It is also the headquarters of the bureau that oversees the GLONASS satellite system, which is the Soviet, now Russian, attempt to duplicate our GPS system. As you recall, under the Soviets, the KGB controlled all of the nuclear weapons. Now that control is delegated to another intelligence bureau. Our sources rode the train in the normal course all the way to Vladivostok where they caught a ship for Nagoya. This priceless piece of information gave us enough of a lead that we were able to alert our port watcher in Vladivostok to watch for the containers. Luckily for us, he spotted them being loaded onto a freighter in the harbor. Sadly, he was compromised the next day and shot by one of the Russian Intelligence Service's men. We believe that the Russians did not realize that he observed the loading of the trigger containers and that they killed him because of things he had done previously. He was not able to report to us the name of the freighter, but is believed that the freighter left the port last Wednesday, the seventh. Our experts estimate the steaming time for that class of freighter to Bushehr is thirty-six days, a day less to Bandar Abbas.

I want you three to head up an operation to find the ship at sea, disable the devices in such a way that the Iranians will not know that they have been tampered with, and let them go on their way to be delivered to the Iranians, or, failing that, destroy the devices or dump them where a deep submersible might be able to recover them.

The reason I want you three to accomplish this for me and not use the military, is that I believe we have a spy in the White House. I am very apprehensive about communications, even by scrambled telephone or encrypted emails. If I involve the military, too many people will have to know. I realize that this constrains you substantially, so I have put a substantial deposit in an account in Banc Suisse in Geneva and you will find three debit cards that can draw on that account in one of the files I am sending with you. You can use the funds to hire the personnel you need and pay expenses.

Once you formulate a plan, I want you to contact me by phone and give the name of Lee Fitzcharles. Leave a message saying that you can be reached at the usual number. Do not give a number. I will call from my limo to one of the cell phones I am enclosing in this pouch. The phones have the numbers one, two and three on them, for you, Jean and Jefe. Sorry to superimpose this complication on your planning and execution, but we are stuck with the facts we have. I have to assume that the culprit works for our direst enemy or enemies, so caution is required.

Janice and I wish you Godspeed. God Bless America.

Fred"

"Whew," said Lero, to himself. By the time he glanced at the photos taken by the agent in Vladivostok and read the report that was dictated over a cell phone by the agent on the train, it was time to call Jean.

"Are you coming along with the computer and screen?" he asked.

"Yes, I will be ready for you to help me lug it to the car when you come. Are you ready to leave?"

"Yes, I will be out of here in five minutes."

"Okay, see you then."

Chapter 3

When he pulled into the parking lot, she was at the garage door on the right side of the shop building. He went in and helped her lug the boxes of gear to the Cherokee. The screen was one of the newer devices and heavier, too, but they managed and drove home with the gear.

Lero backed into their driveway to give a little privacy and to get closer to the door. Once they had lugged the gear into the house and set it on the dining room table, they changed into their casual clothes and fixed dinner.

They spent the evening studying the files and later played the first of the CDs. It was compiled by the Defense Intelligence Agency and given directly and personally to the President. It was not shared with any other Agency. The head of the DIA was Admiral Charles Bostock, an old friend of the President, from their college days. President Thompson had told Lero that Bostock was one of the very few people in upper positions in the intelligence community that he trusted implicitly.

Admiral Bostock's voice narrated the first CD, but he did not identify himself. It was a review of the known facilities in the Iranian Nuclear Program. Pictures taken from ground level as well as satellite photos were used in the presentation. The narrator showed the progress in each facility with a series of satellite photos. The expansion was impressive. Near the end of the CD, there was a report about the mysterious tremor in the mine southeast of Esfahan. Pictures of the area before and after the tremor were displayed next to each other. One could easily observe the sunken, roughly circular area that began near the mouth of the worked out mine and extended several hundred yards up the slope of the mountain. The Narrator said that the "after" photographs were taken two weeks after the tremor from an altitude of ninety statute miles. The sunken center of the crater was a telltale sign of a massive underground explosion. There were no linear clefts or fault lines that might have accompanied an earthquake of that magnitude.

After viewing the CD, they decided that they had had enough for one day. They had worked from early morning until after ten at night.

As they undressed to get into their pajamas, there was a time when both were nude contemporaneously. Lero reached for her arm and pulled her gently to him and hugged her thoroughly. Then he drew back and kissed her warmly. They could feel each press against the other. She was so warm that he decided that he would not let her go, so he backed up to the bed and pulled her next to him as he lay back. She used a hand to cushion her arrival on the bed. For a moment, their eyes met. She looked so beautiful in the dim light from the bathroom door. He looked her directly in the eyes and said, "I love you, Jean." She said, "I love you, Dan."

Later, she lay partly on his chest, with her left leg between his spread legs. Her face was nuzzled into his neck. They fell asleep without moving.

Chapter 4

At the breakfast table, after his eggs and sausage and toast, Lero could not wait any longer to call Jefe. The satellite phone moaned, and groaned and clicked and then rang. This time, Jefe answered with a clearly alert voice.

"Good morning, what is the good word?" he asked.

"Houston," said Lero. "What is your good word?"

"Sedona," said Jefe. Now they both knew they were indeed talking to the person intended.

"What's up?" asked Jefe.

"New project. Eyes only. Cannot brief you now, but you are definitely in on this one. Do you have any contacts in the shipping business?"

"Sure, here in the Greek Isles, there are several international shipping companies, both Greek and otherwise. I have a few contacts. What do you want to know?"

"I need to know the names and descriptions of ships that would have left Vladivostok last Tuesday, Wednesday or Thursday."

"That is an unusual request, but our business deals in the unusual, doesn't it?"

"Yes, it does."

"I will make a few calls and get back to you. Alita sends her best regards. Hope we can see you guys sometime soon."

"Me, too. Thanks, Jefe. Talk to you soon."

"Okay. Bye."

"Was that your friend Lero?" asked Alita, as she shaded her eyes with her left hand.

"Yes. He wanted me to get him some information."

"Can it wait until you put some lotion on me?" she asked teasingly as she rolled over onto her belly on the air mattress they kept by the pool. It was the perfect time of the day to take in the Greek sunlight. She had taken the usual precaution of leaving her clothing on the chair next to him in the shade of the umbrella in the center of the table. He picked up the squeeze bottle of lotion, dropped his shorts by his chair and strode over to help her protect her lovely hips from the dangers of too much sun.

Chapter 5

The telephone on Andrea's desk rang twice. He picked it up. He answered, "Palos Shipping, Andrea Stavrouk speaking."

The familiar voice on the other end said, "Hey there, are you having a good day?"

"Hello, yourself. Yes, I am having a good day. Are you in town? Would you like to join me for lunch?"

"Alas, no, I am not in town. I would love to have joined you for lunch. Perhaps next trip."

"In that case, may I be of service to you, my friend?"

"Yes. I would like to have the names and descriptions of ships that departed Vladivostok last Tuesday, Wednesday and Thursday, with destinations, too, please."

"Formidable!!" (in French), he said. "That is a tall order. I will have to access our 'special network' to retrieve that information. There will be a delay and I will need some lubricant to smooth the way."

"I am so grateful to you and your special network. Tell me how much to send and I will mail you a money order. Add enough for your expenses, too, my friend."

He thought for a minute, and said, "There will be at least two other people involved. I will need Four Thousand Drachmas to accomplish what you wish."

"I will mail the money order today to your post office box. Email your results to 'bigchief48@aol.com,' please."

"I will send the results promptly. It may take a day or two. Thank you for allowing me to be of service."

"Thank you, Andrea. You are such a big help to me when I need help. I wish we could see each other more often. Give my best regards to Elena, please."

"Thank you, too. Take care of yourself, my friend. Goodbye."

"Goodbye, my friend."

The old black clanging telephone rang in the office of Daivin Forwarding Company in Kowloon.

"Mr. Wu's office," came the soothing greeting from a female voice.

"Good afternoon," said Andrea, "May I speak to Mr. Wu, please. Andrea Stavrouk with Palos Shipping in Pireaus, Greece, is calling."

"Ah, Mr. Stavrouk, he is just concluding a meeting with buyers, if you can hold, I will tell him you are calling."

"Thank you."

A minute passed. Long distance tolls are not as punitive as they used to be, so Andrea waited patiently.

"Mr. Stavrouk, how nice to hear from you. How can I be of service today?" asked Chao Wu.

"I was wondering, with your vast contacts, if you could determine for me the list of departures from Vladivostok on last Tuesday, Wednesday and Thursday."

"Ah, my friend, I may be able to achieve that, but I will have to operate through an intermediary. There will be some expense. Would your requesting party be willing to invest Two Thousand Honk Kong dollars in such a project?" he asked.

"I am sure he would be willing. When you have the data, just call me and I will wire the fees to the account you wish," said Andrea.

"I will try to get that information for you right away. When do you foresee that you will have time to visit us in person again, my friend?" asked Wu.

"Thank you, Wu. I would love to visit again soon. You must advise me if you ever come out this way. I would be glad to see you and perhaps I can return the favor you accorded me by introducing you to one of our

Greek ladies. I will never forget the pleasures I experienced with your friend the last time I was in Hong Kong. I will await your call. Thank you again."

"You are welcome, my friend. Talk to you again soon."

Wu hesitated only a moment after he hung up with Andrea before he dialed a lengthy international number.

There was considerable hesitation on the line. Then a gruff voice answered in Russian, "Strasweche (phonetic). (Hello.) Harbor Master, Sergeant Sergeivitch."

"This is Mr. Wu with Daivin Forwarding Company in Kowloon. I wish to speak with Captain Margolin, please."

"One moment. Hold, please."

"This is Captain Margolin, Mr. Wu, how are you, my friend?"

"I am fine, Captain, how are you today?"

"I am good. Healthy as a horse, as they say. How may I be of assistance?"

"An associate wishes the departure records for last Tuesday, Wednesday and Thursday for his records. His subordinates foolishly failed to keep these records while the big boss was off on holiday. They wish to replace them before he finds out."

"Such records are closely held. It will require some lubricant to wrest them from unwilling hands, my friend," said Margolin.

"How much lubricant would be required, my friend?" asked Wu.

"I think five hundred rubles would be enough," said Margolin.

"When you fax the data, I will deposit that amount in the account we previously used, if that is acceptable."

"That would be fine, my friend. You must visit again soon. We have new girls in town since your last visit."

"Ah, the last visit was most memorable. I will look forward to another visit, perhaps in the spring."

"I hope so. I will fax the information as soon as received. If there is a complication, I will call you. Thank you for allowing us to be of service."

"Good to talk with you again, Yuri. See you later," said Wu and then he hung up.

A quick call by Margolin to the harbormaster's secretary got him the information he wanted. Of course, he had to exchange an envelope with fifty rubles in it for the envelope with the three sheets of information in it.

Tanya was an excellent source and an efficient associate in such matters. Yuri remembered to slip one of the latest catalogs from Fredericks of Hollywood into the envelop he gave her. She squealed with glee later when she opened it. "Yuri can be so thoughtful," she thought.

The quiet private network operated on trust and generous enrichment. It had taken years for Wu to set up both ends and it worked like a well-oiled machine. There were no slip ups and everyone was satisfied with the arrangement.

Chapter 6

As the wheels of international commerce were turning, Alita awakened on the air mattress beside the pool and rolled over to awaken Jefe. She raised up without waking him and sat down on him, just so, his favorite wake up call. He, of course, awakened immediately and reached for her, gallantly keeping her from falling by cradling her tanned, oily breasts in each hand. She slowly lowered herself onto him and kissed him like she had not seen him for a long time.

Through the kitchen window, the housekeeper, Maria, observed all this ceremony with indifference. She was giving all her attention to the crab salad, soft rolls and lemonade she was preparing for their lunch by the pool. She knew Jefe would sometime soon put on his robe and come in to get the tray. She would then be free to tidy up the place a bit and stay out of their way during the afternoon. By mid-afternoon, she would be finished for the day and would leave quietly using her key to lock the door and let herself out the locked gate at the end of the driveway.

Chapter 7

Lero mused as he drove the short distance from Jean's house to his office building. The Jeep carried him quietly. He kept the radio turned off, so he could think without distraction. Many questions occurred to him as he swept along the perimeter road and across the fields of mothballed aircraft. The Jeep and he arrived soon enough at his office building. When Jefe told President Thompson that he wanted to ease into retirement, the President did not hesitate to put Lero in charge of the unit. Velma stayed on, like the fixture she was, and he was so glad she did. It is said that the sergeants run the military, but he knew that without Velma, he would be quite handicapped. He wondered what he would do when she decided to retire, too. He resolved to give some thought to asking her to pick and train her replacement before she retired. Her white Toyota was in the parking lot as he drove in. It was already over eighty degrees on what promised to be another scorcher in Tucson. He used his electronic key fob to unlock the door and opened it with his key hand. Just inside, he was shocked to see Velma stretched out on the floor, her key fob still in her hand. He was shocked into motionless for a few seconds. Then he moved quickly to feel for a pulse in her left wrist. There was none. She was gone. She had not even turned the lights on, so he did.

He immediately took out his cell phone and dialed.

"Base security, Sergeant Hodges speaking."

"This is Mr. Roman in Building 413. My secretary has collapsed. Bring the defibrillator and send an ambulance, please. Hurry."

"Right away, sir. We are rolling."

Lero put his phone down beside Velma and felt again for a pulse. She was quite still and there was no pulse. The shock of finding her like this set in. He sobbed and said, "Velma, I am so sad to have you leave like this. Lord bless her and keep her."

It only took forty five seconds for the ambulance to arrive from the Medical Unit. It was only a half mile away. Two technicians in white shirts and khaki pants hustled in from the ambulance. Lero looked up from his position on his knees next to her and rose to give them access. He went over to a chair by the conference table and sat down heavily. He watched as they turned her over and pulled her blouse apart enough to put the paddles on her chest. She jerked as they used the defibrillator. One put his stethoscope against her chest.

He nodded negatively and they hit her again with the defibrillator. She jerked again. The corpsman listened again but found no pulse. He looked up at Lero and sadly nodded again. They tried a third time, but it was no use. Velma was gone.

Lero was stunned. He had only known Velma for about two years, but she was like a mother and older sister to him and the whole crew at the unit. Now, they had lost their polar star.

He dialed Jean.

"Hello," she said, without identifying her unit or name, which was standard procedure for her.

"I found Velma, unconscious on the floor when I came in. The paramedics are working on her now," he said.

"Oh, how awful," Jean said. "Do you want me to come?"

"Not just yet. I don't know where they will take her."

Sensing the heaviness in his voice, she asked, "How bad is it?"

"It's bad," said Lero, choking.

"I am on my way," she said and hung up without waiting for his reply.

In a minute, she pulled into the parking lot, got out of the car and trotted into the building. The paramedics were just ready to wheel Velma out. They had put an oxygen mask on her and started oxygen, and wheeled her out just as Jean got to the door. Lero saw Jean arrive and went over to her. They hugged for a long time. Seemingly within seconds, the ambulance was gone with Velma. The place seemed so empty. They sat at the conference table for a several minutes. Neither spoke. They both knew that Velma was gone. Jean reached over and put a consoling hand on his. Their eyes met, both full of tears. In combat, there is no time for grief, sometimes. Here, where no one was shooting at them, the shock and grief could be allowed. They sat for a long time.

After a while, the phone rang. "Building four one three," he answered.

"Mr. Roman, this is Doctor Polanski at the infirmary. I regret to inform you that Mrs. Weber had expired. I am sorry."

"I understand, Dr. Polanski. Thank you for calling. I will call your office later when I sort things out."

"Very well. I am sorry for your loss."

Lero hung up. They sat in silence some more.

Chapter 8

Lero and Jean went over to Velma's desk. He had to over-ride the key pad to get access. They went to the locked file cabinet and did the same. In the file cabinet were the personnel files. Each person was permitted to place an envelope in their file "just in case." Jean retrieved Velma's personnel file and they sat at the conference table to review it.

It showed that she was an only child. Parents deceased. Born in Toledo, Ohio, in nineteen forty eight. Bachelors from Willimette College. Career Air Force. Intelligence Units, mostly in the Washington, D.C. area. Contracted by Jefe in twenty oh two. Worked at Davis Monthan since. Never married. No children.

In her file, also, was her Last Will and Testament. They were surprised to find that she left her entire estate to Jean, Lero and Jefe (real names omitted as classified), for projects they chose. There was an envelope on which she had written "Arrangments."

"I want my body to be cremated. In the years that I have spent in Tucson, I have learned to love the dry desert climate. I want Lero, Jean and Jefe, to choose a spot to scatter my ashes where they can come when they want to remember me. I have grown so close to them that I consider them my family. It would be some comfort to me to remain close to them. I know it is an imposition on them to see to my final arrangements, but I know they will do as I direct, with tenderness. Goodbye, my friends. I have loved working with you and admiring your devotion to duty. Keep me in your hearts as I will keep you in mine."

Neither Lero nor Jean could speak for a while.

Lero walked to his desk in the inner office. He picked up the satellite phone and dialed a familiar number. It buzzed, moaned, clicked and then rang the number dialed.

"Hello," came the familiar voice.

"This is Lero, say the word."

"Sedona. What is your good word?"

"Houston."

"What's up?" he asked.

"What is your twenty (location)? Asked Lero.

"Station two (meaning his place on Keros)."

"Are you able to talk freely?" asked Lero.

"Yes, I am alone. Alita is taking a nap."

"I have bad news."

"What?"

"It's Velma. I found her in the office this morning. She's gone."

"Oh, my," said Jefe. There was a long pause.

When he finally spoke, his voice was cracking.

"How?"

"I found her sprawled on the office floor, just inside the door. It looks like she had a stroke or heart attack or something else sudden. It looked like she just fell over onto the floor. I found her when I came in this morning about an hour and a half ago. The paramedics came quickly and tried defibrillating, but it was no use. Nothing appears to have been disturbed in the office. I am confident that security was not breached, but I will view the surveillance tapes and let you know if anything appears. Let me just talk and you listen. We went through her personnel file. She wanted to be cremated and you and Jean and I are in charge of choosing a spot to scatter her ashes. Think about that and let me know if you have a thought. I don't know how soon the medical examiner will release her, but I will make the arrangements here. She had no family, parents deceased, no siblings or children. I will arrange an obituary in the paper. Can you think of anyone we should notify?"

"No," Jefe's voice croaked. "Go ahead and make arrangements. Alita and I will fly in commercial. I will let you know when. Thanks for calling me. I know this is tough for you both, too. See you soon."

Lero forced himself to get out the surveillance tapes and scan them for anything. There was nothing on them, until just before nine o'clock that morning. It showed Velma arriving. It was necessary for the first person in to turn off the surveillance devices and she was only just in the door when the cameras recorded her collapse. When Lero saw himself arrive on the tape, only a couple of minutes later, he turned off the tape.

Jean went back to her office and Lero stayed to take care of some preparations for his own travel and the arrival of Jefe and Alita. Later, he called the only funeral home he knew in town and made arrangements for them to pick up Velma. He instructed the funeral home people to cremate her remains without embalming them. They said they needed a signature from him and asked if he would come by and sign an agreement with them. He said he would come right away and left the office. He took her Last Will and Testament with him. He had been surprised to find that Velma had named him executor and Jean as alternate executor.

Chapter 9

When he arrived at Wilson's Funeral Home, he was shown into the office by a lady who closed the door behind him. Mr. Wilson, a large man of about fifty years of age, greeted him warmly with a handshake from a huge hand.

"I am so sorry for your loss, Mr. Roman. Please sit down and tell me how we can be of service."

"I was surprised to be named Executor of her will, Mr. Wilson, but Velma wanted to be cremated without being embalmed and her ashes scattered at a place to be chosen by me, her friend Jean and her friend (note: this name will appear as Jefe, but his actual name will be withheld for security reasons)."

"We can take care of that right away for you, Mr. Roman. Where is she now?"

"At Dr. Polanski's facility at Davis Monthan Air Base. I will tell him to expect you."

"Would you like to choose an urn at this time?" asked Mr. Wilson.

"Yes. That would remove some of the burden on others," said Lero.

"Come with me and we will show you our selection. If you don't find one that fits your needs, we can order one from a large collection and have it here tomorrow."

Lero and Mr. Wilson went to the display room, where Lero chose a plain, but dignified light blue urn.

When they returned to Mr. Wilson's office, Lero asked if he would like a deposit on the fees.

"That is not necessary. I know there are lots of details for you to attend to right now. We will bring a statement when we deliver the urn. We will call first if you will give me a number."

"Can you give me an approximate amount, so I can be prepared?" asked Lero.

"Sure. Let's see. Pickup at Dr. Polanski's office; transport to our crematory, placing of remains in urn, cremation fee, transportation to your office. It should be somewhere between Nine hundred fifty dollars and a thousand. Does that seem satisfactory to you?"

"Yes, that is fine. Thank you. You have helped me get through this as painlessly as possible."

"That is what we are here for, Mr. Roman. Again, we are so sorry for your loss. Please let us know if you need anything further. We will bring you six copies of the death certificate with the urn."

"Thank you again, Mr. Wilson. See you later."

It was a quiet meal at Jean's house that night. After dinner, as they were clearing the dishes and putting them in the dishwasher, Lero said, "Jefe and Alita are coming as soon as they can pack and get a flight. I would expect to see them sometime tomorrow. We need to decide whether to pick a place to scatter Velma's ashes or whether to wait until later to do that. Since she didn't have relatives, we are, or were, her family. I think we should do something to commemorate her life. What do you think?"

"My initial idea is to scatter her ashes near the center of the active runway some sunny day. That way, we will always have her with us and she will always be close to us and what she loved doing so much."

"I think that is a great idea. Let's suggest that to Jefe when they arrive."

Jefe and Alita were able to get a flight from Athens to New York and a connecting flight to Phoenix Sky Harbor. They ate a sad dinner looking out the window at their swimming pool and deck, saddened by the loss of their friend Velma and saddened by the knowledge that it would be a while before they could bask in the Greek sunlight by the pool. Jefe thought putting suntan lotion on Alita's naked hips would be something he would never forget.

Jefe called the sea taxi and got on the schedule to be picked up at the harbor in town. The next trip would leave at nine P.M. They could nap a bit on the boat and get to Athens near dawn. He planned to drive them to the harbor in their ancient Hillman Minx and leave it there for Maria to pick up and return to their villa. He pondered how quickly he could get from Keros to Tucson, and then pondered that it seemed like a long time.

Alita asked Jefe, "Is there something else brewing with you and Lero? You seem a bit preoccupied."

"Yes, he has a serious problem. I may have to stay in Tucson for a while to help him and Jean. There is no time to bring a new person up to speed and we need to move fast."

"How can I help?" she asked.

"Just stay by my side and do what you can. I would especially appreciate it if you would sleep next to me in your Greek tan. You know how it calms me," he grinned.

"I would not have described it as 'calming,' my dear, but it would be my pleasure to comfort you."

They share a meaningful kiss from adjacent chairs at the kitchen table.

In two hours, they had packed, secured things at the villa and we ready to carry baggage to the car. Jefe had a cart he liked to use for the purpose. He had liked the fact that the villa was on one floor. Actually it was hewn out of the native stone and levelled by the workers who built the villa when they installed the tile floors throughout. Jefe left a thorough note for Maria on the kitchen table to tell her where he was going and why and that he would send her a fax message when he needed to. He told her it might be months before they could return to Keros.

The little Hillman was full of luggage as they went out the gate, locked it, and went down the curving road along the face of the mountain to the seashore and the harbor. He hired a porter to lug their bags to the wharf where the sea taxi would dock. Once emptied, he parked the Hillman in the lot and locked it carefully. He gave it an affectionate pat as he turned to walk back to wait with Alita.

Chapter 10

Lero dialed his regular phone. After a few odd noises and rings, a lady with a British accent answered.

"Brighton Marine Insurance, may I help you?"

"May I speak to Alistair Burton, please, Mr. Dan Roman calling."

"One moment, please, I will see if he is available."

She had him on hold for half a minute, then a male voice came on.

"Dan. Wow, long time no see. How are you? Where are you? What are you doing? Catch me up."

"Thanks for taking my call, Al. I am fine. I am in the states, actually in Arizona. I am working with a consulting company and I could use some of your expertise."

"Sure, Dan. How can I help?"

"My people are trying to locate a ship that departed Vladivostok last Tuesday, Wednesday or Thursday. At this time, we believe it is bound for Singapore. I need to know how to go about finding the ship at sea."

"Wow, that is a problem, isn't it. There are approximately fifteen thousand commercial ships at sea at any given time. If they are still using their transponder, it should not be too hard to find it, with satellite information and all. What is the ship's name?"

"That is just it, Al. All I know about it is that it departed Vladivostok. I don't know its name or registration."

"Well, if it switched off its transponder, it could be a needle in a haystack. That is one of the busiest shipping lanes in the world. Eighty percent of Asian traffic passes through the Malacca Straits. That might be the best place to spot it. If we knew its steaming speed, I could tell you when it might reach the Straits."

"It would be a guess, Al. What would the average freighter make?"

"The average would be about twelve knots, but it could be somewhat less than that or substantially more."

"Let me ask you this. If we assume twelve knots, when would it reach the Malacca Straits?"

"Roughly calculating, it would reach the eastern end of the straits in five and a half days. But like I said, it could be more or less."

"You have been very helpful. May I call you again for a consultation if I need further information? Please run a tab and send me a bill for this. I can give you the address."

"I will run a tab, as you say. If this is personal, no charge, my friend. If it is business, I will open an account in your name and we can settle up later."

"It is business, Al, but I really appreciate the help. I will be in touch. My address in Tucson is 123 Sunset Court. I will call you again soon, I think."

"Take care, Dan. It was nice to hear your voice. Are you still flying any?"

"Just private time in a Twin Comanche."

"Well, keep the blue side up and see you soon."

"Thanks again, Al. Bye."

"Bye."

Chapter 11

The Grand Ayatollah was finishing some tedious planning near the end of his office hours when his secretary, Yosuf, entered and said that General Arak wished to see him.

"Show him in," said the Grand Ayatollah.

Arak entered in a moment or two. He was fifty-ish, slender with dark, deep set eyes and a nose that was a bit too big and too pointed for his face.

"Your Excellency, so good to see you again."

"Wadeh, so good to see you also. Are you well?"

"Yes, praise Allah, I have almost totally recovered from the surgery. I trust you are well, Excellency."
"Yes, I am well. What did you want to discuss today?"

"I have come to tell you that that little project you put in my hands is under way. The ship sailed just after midnight the night of Tuesday/Wednesday. We estimate it will make port in thirty six days. Per your instructions they are running in the black without any transponder to avoid any detection. We do not expect to hear from them again until they sail into the harbor."

"That is as good as we could hope for. Have our investigators determined what happened in the desert last month?"

"No, Excellency. We are still running tests, but the overburden is so deep and the site so remote that you may choose not to pursue the matter further due to the expense."

"Wise of you to see that, Wadeh. We must not only husband our assets carefully, but any major excavation at the site would be immediately visible to the infidels. Please keep me informed and alert me when you expect to receive the ship."

"I shall see to it personally, Excellency," said General Arak, who saluted and turned on his heel on the lush carpet and left the office.

Chapter 12

Lero was sitting at his desk, once again. It seemed strange to not have Velma in the outer office. Her presence always gave him a sense of things being in control, even in the most hectic of circumstances. Because he was working alone, he left the door to his office open. He heard the fax machine come on and answer the incoming call. Then, after a pause, the copier feature energized and paper began to roll out. The sheet feed was dropping the second sheet before he got out to the fax machine. The header said "Brighton Marine Insurance." He waited until the full message was printed and picked up the sheaf of papers and went to the window to examine them in the better light.

The letter was addressed to Mr. Dan Roman, 123 Sunset Place, Tucson, Arizona. The sender was listed as a long international phone number.

The letter read, "Hey Dan, So good to hear from you after such a long time. Glad that things are going well for you. I was so sorry to hear about Martha. After the airline fell out from under us, I guess we guys scattered to the four winds. I ended up here in Plymouth, England, and, through the best of good fortune, got this job with Brighton. It allows me to travel some, which I really enjoy. I met a local lady and have settled down here.

I am transmitting a list of ships that departed the harbor you mentioned, on the dates you mentioned, with gross tonnages which might help you discriminate the ship you are seeking. Registries are included, too, but they really don't mean much. Shipping companies register their ships in the country that gives them the best deal and hassles them the least about safety, etc. Caution, also, that the language of the name cannot be relied upon to indicate the nation of the owner or owners. Many freighters are owned quietly and the owners avoid any public exposure when they can.

Keep me in touch and let me know any time you are in the vicinity. It would be great to see you.

Best wishes,

Al

Allister Burton

Forwarding Manager

The next page listed the ships and dates of departure.

The Tuesday list was:

Hiroku Maru, 15000 tonnes, destination Nagoya, Japanese Registry.

November Victory (translated from Russian), 16000 tonnes, destination Singapore, Russian Registry.

Mandrakos Aigle, 14000 tonnes, Destination Tyre, Greek Registry

Wednesday departures:

Sir James Wheaton, 18000 tonnes, Destination Liverpool, British Registry.

Belle Dame Sans Mercie, 15000 tonnes, Destination Marseilles, Algerian Registry.

Thursday departures:

Ton Son Nhut, 17000 tonnes, Destination Ho Chi Minh City, Vietnamese Registry

Santa Ana de Bordo, 14000 tonnes, Destination Havana, Cuban Registry.

Lero carried the papers back to his desk. He turned to his desktop PC and typed in "IHS Maritime and Trade. He had been advised by Jefe a while ago to subscribe to their service. It could locate a ship anywhere in the world and at least tell the inquirer where it was docked or from which port it last sailed. This was the first time in a long time that Lero had had to use this site and he struggled for a bit until he got the swing of things.

His first assumption was that the destinations listed by the ships that had departed Vladivostok could be accurate or bogus. However, he could locate the legitimate ships by their transponders and thus probably narrow the field of "bogies" to two or so.

After an hour's study, he eliminated all but the Ton Son Nhut and the November Victory from suspicion. Since they departed six and eight days ago, they could be quite a way from the port. Another suspicious fact was that neither was operating its transponder. The oceans of the world cover two thirds of the globe. Now he had two ships out there somewhere, and one had three nuclear triggers in its belly.

Chapter 13

Jefe and Alita arrived at three PM the next day. Lero and Jean went to pick them up at Sky Harbor. The four were glad to see each other, but the greeting was overshadowed by the sadness of Velma's death. Nobody spoke much as they drove the desert highway back to Tucson. Lero and Jean dropped Jefe and Alita at his place and agreed to come back and have dinner with them that evening.

As they were leaving for dinner, Jean looked smashing in a blue dress and heels. Lero constantly marveled at how beautiful she was. He wore his new sport coat and slacks and they looked like your average American couple, only more handsome. She noticed his admiring look and came closer and gave him a tender smooch.

"My goodness, you are beautiful," he said.

"I am so glad you think so," she said as they walked to the door. The desert heat hit them like a fly swatter as they walked the fifty feet to the Grand Cherokee.

It was a ten minute drive from Jean's house to Jefe's. His Spanishesque house was in a fashionable subdivision and was set back from the road about fifty feet. There was a perimeter fence from each side of the house that extended back to surround the back yard and their swimming pool.

The doorbell chimed softly and in about ten seconds, Alita answered it. The mild aroma of cooking odors followed her from the kitchen. She waved them into the kitchen where Jefe sat on a stool at the island in the middle. He smiled and offered them a drink and they picked ice tea and lemonade. (Note: Neither Jefe nor Lero drink any alcohol. A long standing professional sacrifice, but they both believed that the daily ingestion of ethanol dulls the senses.)

Once they were seated, Jefe asked Lero about the arrangements for Velma. Lero reviewed the arrangements he had made with Mr. Wilson and told Jefe and Alita that Velma's will named him as Executor and Jean as Alternate Executor. He reviewed the arrangements that Velma had left in her personnel file. Jefe asked them if they had a suggestion about where to scatter Velma's ashes and when they might want to do that. Lero told Alita and Jefe about Jean's suggestion that they scatter Velma's ashes on the center line of the active runway. It seemed appropriate to them, too, and they agreed for the time being that they would plan on doing it that way.

Lero dialed the Davis Monthan Tower.

"Tower, Darwin speaking."

"Buddy, this is Dan Roman in building 413. We would like clearance to take the courtesy car to the center of Runway One Two tomorrow about noon to scatter Velma's ashes. We will not delay traffic, but it may take us ten minutes."

"Dan, all the guys are so sorry about Velma. Please accept our condolences. Request approved. Have the lineman call on the telephone or Unicom when he wants to go out. We will hold traffic if necessary. Take your time."

"Thanks, Buddy. We appreciate that. Talk to you later."

Dinner was chicken fajitas, with sauteed green peppers and onions and rice and just enough garlic. The aroma was delightful and the makings were spread out around the platter of chopped chicken. Jefe had just gotten a nice wedge of parmesan cheese and he used his rotary shredder to give each person a generous covering. As good as the food was, the mood was somber.

They agreed to meet at noon the next day at the office and go from there to the Fixed Base Operator's building where the lineman would take them to the center of the active runway in the courtesy car.

Chapter 14

The next day, Jefe and Alita came to the office just before noon. Jean drove down and met them there. They all piled into the Grand Cherokee. Jean drove. Lero took the passenger seat and held the urn. No one spoke as they drove to the fixed base operator's building.

When they walked in, there were about fifty people waiting to convey their sympathies and bid goodbye to Velma. Jean and Lero and Jefe and Alita all circulated among the friends and exchanged tears and hugs. Then it was time to go. Eddie had called the tower and was holding the door for them. They walked slowly to the car. Unknown to Lero and the others, the fixed base operator had gotten clearance for a large crowd, with vehicles, to go out to the center of the runway. Jason, the FBO, asked Lero and Jefe if they would mind if her friends shared the moment with them. Lero and Jefe both choked.

Buddy was watching from the tower. As the procession made ready to go out onto the runway, he broadcast in the open. "Attention all aircraft. Runway One Two at Davis Monthan is closed temporarily. Will advise when it reopens. Contact Approach control on one two five decimal seven for advisories."

In all there were six carloads of people. The tower gave Eddie clearance to go onto the active runway and stood by to hold any approaching or departing traffic. Eddie stopped the Suburban on the mid stripe near the center of Runway Twelve and the solemn procession got out and gathered behind Lero and Jefe and Jean and Alita.

Before they opened the urn, Jefe addressed the unexpected assembly.

"All of you are here to say goodbye to our friend, Velma. She was a good worker, a good soldier, a good friend who could be counted on absolutely. I worked with Velma back east for several years before we were transferred here. I guess I have known her for twenty five years. In all that time, she never hesitated to get her job done and to be cheerful about it. We had some difficult assignments and lost some mutual friends. I would like to say a brief prayer."

"Lord, we are here today to scatter the ashes of our dear friend Velma. In doing this, we believe she will always be close to us and part of us. She loved this place and she loved her work. She was a devoted friend. We ask that you bless and keep her. Make your face to shine upon her. Lift up your countenance upon her and grant her your Peace, and keep her kindly, gently, and safely in the palm of your hand."

There was a complete silence. Strangely, there were no airplane noises, just silence. Lero opened the urn and began to walk away from the crowd down the center stripe, spilling Velma's ashes out as he went. When he was certain the ashes were completely dispersed, he turned and walked back to the crowd.

When he got within a few feet of the silent group, he said, "Thank you so much for coming to this ceremony. It would have meant a lot to Velma and it means a lot to us. We will never forget you, Velma."

Then, the solemn group got back into their vehicles. When they got back to the FBO, a C-141 was just departing Runway 12. They all stopped and watched it rotate about two thirds of the way down the runway and climb into the sun. It was fitting.

Chapter 15

Later, back at the office, Lero dialed a familiar number.

"President Thompson's office."

"This is Lee Fitzcharles. Would you ask the President to call me at his convenience?"

"Yes, Mr. Fitzcharles. Does he have your number?"

"Yes, ma'am, he does. Thank you."

"Very well. Good day," she said and the line went silent.

It was nine thirty that evening when one of the cell phones rang. Lero immediately turned the TV down and walked over to pick it up and answered.

"Hello."

"Hello, is this Mr. Fitzcharles?" asked the familiar voice.

"Yes it is."

"Say the word, please."

"Houston."

"What is up?"

"Our best information is that two candidates are the best choices. Other candidates have been found to be very low probability. We are ready to begin our hunting trip. Turkeys can be very skittish and must be stalked very carefully."

"I understand. You will need a security code for this hunting trip. Let's call it Turkey Hunt. I will notify my contact in the DIA (Defense Intelligence Agency) so you will be able to travel on military aircraft and vessels and draw such equipment as you need. Will you be hiring a guide for the turkey hunt?"

"Yes, sir. The area we intend to hunt is large enough that we feel we may need as many as twenty hunters for a proper drive."

"That is fine with me. Keep me in the loop, please."

"Of course, sir."

"I will have a better evening now, knowing that you are organizing the turkey hunt. Good hunting."

"Thank you, sir. Good evening."

The line went silent.

Chapter 16

In the morning, before it got too hot, Jefe arrived at the Quonset hut office. When he walked in, he was struck by the absence of Velma and it saddened him.

Lero saw him come in the front door and came out to greet him.

"I find it is best not to look at the empty desk just now," he said to his solemn friend.

"Right. Let's go into your office."

Lero and Jefe sat down at the conference table. There were papers in neat piles under a gray blanket.

It was a strange moment for them. Jefe had sat with Lero many times at the same table when Jefe was the head of the unit, but now, Jefe was retired and Lero was head of the unit.

Lero said, "I asked Mr. Murfree to let me bring you into something. Are you up to getting back in harness for a while. I really need you."

"Sure, I really miss the work. Retirement is nice, but I miss what we used to do together. What is the assignment?"

Lero pulled back the gray blanket and launched into a full briefing. He spoke for about twenty minutes without stopping, explaining the problems and what the President wanted the unit to do about them. He reviewed the communication protocol due to the suspicion of a mole in the White House and Jefe nodded solemnly.

Jefe whistled softly and asked, "Have you formulated a plan?"

"I am at the formulating stage. Velma's death has caused all of us to take a pause. I would not have done it any other way, but now we need to move. Do you think we can proceed without being disrespectful?"

"Velma would have been the first to tell you to get a move on. Where do we start?"

"Well, we have narrowed our search to two suspected freighters that left Vladivostok on Tuesday and Thursday. They both make about the same speed. We think they will take the shortest route to Disneyland and make port at Bandar Abbas. We need to put together a crew of operators to find those ships, get out to them, board them and disable those triggers without detection or destroy or jettison them if we cannot disable them without detection. We need air and sea transportation and a crew of operators. I told

Mr. Murfree that we would need twenty persons and he is fine with that. We have private funds and debit cards to draw on it from the Banc Suisse in Geneva. We have a military operation name – Turkey Hunt, so we can requisition what we need in the way of equipment and transportation. Who do you think we should get to build a team?"

"Let's call General McKay. He is retired and will know some fellow retirees who can help us. If we can keep the team small, all the quieter."

"Good," said Lero and got up to get General McKay's phone number. He had just gotten to that file in his desktop computer, when Jefe said, "I found his number in my phone. Do you want to call him on your phone and put it on speaker?"

He called the digits to Lero who dialed and they both sat at Lero's desk while the phone rang.

"I had this place swept yesterday, so I think we are okay," he said.

"Can't be too careful," said Jefe.

(For those who missed it earlier, Jefe's real name is Harry Brubaker. For those of you with a penchant for military and literary history, you will notice that there was an aviator with the same name in the Michener book, "The Bridges at Toko Ri." Pure coincidence.)

"Hello,"came the greeting from the phone and through the speaker.

"General this is Lero with Jefe on a speaker phone. Do you have time to talk with us for a bit?"

"Sure thing, nice to hear from you both. What is your twenty?"

"We are at our headquarters at Davis Monthan."

"I see. Currently I am on a fishing trip on the Mobjack Bay with family and friends. The background noise is sufficient to give us enough privacy. What is up?"

"Think the elves from Disneyland have purchased some mushroom seeds from Ivan and are transporting them by ship from Vladivostok to Bandar Abbas. One suspected ship left on Tuesday, the other on Thursday. We need a crew to find the ships and then we need a crew to go out and board them, disable the seeds if possible, without detection, and failing that, destroy them or throw them overboard."

There was a silence. Then the General spoke.

"I would recommend you get Sergeant Major Bernie Maroney in Jacksonville, North Carolina to put a team together for you. He recently retired and is current with systems and knows a lot of guys who would love to go turkey hunting. If I can help, my quarters now are in Hampton, Virginia and I can be mobile on short notice."

"Thank you, General. We will be back in touch after we talk to Maroney. I am certain we will want your advice on this thing."

"Okay, talk to you later."

The line went silent.

"I really think we need to get out there. We can get our team to join up with us on the fly, so to speak. We need to be closer to where the action is going to take place."

"Where would you recommend?" asked Lero.

"Singapore would be good. We don't have a military presence anywhere near there, though. How about an aircraft carrier? We could check to see where the nearest one is stationed."

"I like the idea of an aircraft carrier. No land bound entanglements. Long reach if we need to strike. Let's call Admiral Bostock."

Once again, Lero dialed. It was nearly noon on the east coast and Admiral Bostock was fixing lunch with his wife when he answered.

"Bostock residence," he said.

"Admiral, this is Lero. I have Jefe with me on a speaker phone. Can you talk to us for a bit?"

"Sure thing, what's up? Where are you?"

"We are at our headquarters at Davis Monthan. We have an operation going and we need to locate our command and control in the south Pacific. Do we have an aircraft carrier in that area we could use?"

"I will have to make a call or two, but I will get back to you."

"Thanks, Admiral. Best regards. We will await your call."

The line went silent.

Chapter 17

Jefe reached over and dialed another number. After a couple of rings, the answer came, "Pacific Air Ops, Lieutenant Muldoon speaking."

"Lieutenant Muldoon, this is Jefe. Do we have anything going to Clark from the west coast?"

"Just a minute, sir. I will check." The line had a slight buzz.

(Note: The reference to Clark means Clark Air Force Base in the Philipines.)

In a while, he came back.

"Yes, sir. We have a KC-10 departing Vandenberg tomorrow morning, assigned to the Oregon National Guard, going to Clark Air Base for a six month assignment, with a stop at Anderson on, Guam. Do you need a seat, sir?"

"Hold a couple of seats for me, please. I will confirm or release them later today, if that is alright."

"That is fine, sir. How can I reach you if I need to?"

Jefe gave him the desk phone number.

"Thank you, sir, good day."

"Good day, Muldoon. Thanks."

"Will you be gone long?" asked Jean.

"I really don't know. We need to find this vessel and plan our attack and execute. I may be gone for a while."

"What do you want me to do while you are gone?" she asked.

"I want you to forward the phone from your lab to the office and person the office. We need someone there to serve as contact point. You can forward the office phone to your cell number when you are away from the office. Can you do that for us?" he asked.

"Sure," she said. "Was General McKay helpful?"

"You bet. He recommended a fellow that Jefe and I are going to talk to right away. The man is a recently retired Sergeant Major from the Delta Force and a sniper instructor. If we can get him to head up our assault force, we will be in good shape."

Chapter 18

Lero called Admiral Bostock again. After an exchange of pleasantries, Lero asked if Bostock could free up a technician for a "project" "in the black." (Meaning, off the books or secret.) The Admiral said that he could and that he would have a Commander Bannister call Lero. Lero gave Bostock his satellite phone number for the technician to call on.

"Thank you, Admiral. Mr. Murfree recommended we call on you. He has complete confidence in you, sir."

"I appreciate that, Lero. Fred and I go way back. We have remained close over the years. He is a great American."

"I think so, too, sir. Thanks again. I will expect Commander Bannister's call."

When Bannister called, Lero outlined the "project."

"We need to locate two ships in the South China Sea. If we are correct, because they left two days apart, they could be as much as six hundred nautical miles apart. We have their names, but they are running without transponders. Both are at this time southbound and we believe they are headed for the Malacca Straits. Can you help us find them?"

"Yes, we can help. We can use overhead surveillance to locate all the ships in the area that are using their transponders and eliminate them from overhead photographs. This will narrow the search substantially. Once we see what ships are left, we can eliminate some by size, either too big or too small. Once we have that done, we can ask our patrol planes to look for some and our ships in the area to look, too. I can put a crew on this right away. Is this urgent, sir?"

"No, it is not urgent, but it is important. We need quality, not speed. We have enough time in this situation. Now many ships would you estimate are in that area southbound at this time?"

"Based on recent history, I would say a good ballpark figure is three hundred, sir. If your people's estimate is correct, such freighters would not be outbound from the coast, but paralleling it. That would eliminate a lot of ships in the area."

"Our people supplied me with tonnage and length information, only. The first ship is seventeen thousand tons and two hundred ten feet long. The second ship is sixteen thousand tons and two hundred six feet long. One is named Ton Son Nhut, Vietnamese registry and the other is November Victory, Russian registry."

"I will put our best people on this. Do you want a report as soon as we encounter either of them?"

"Yes, night or day. Use this number, please. Good hunting. Thanks again."

"You are welcome, sir. Good day."

Chapter 19

In the middle of the afternoon, Jefe called.

"My people inform me that we have a carrier, the Reagan, in the south China Sea, approximately three hundred nautical southwest of Taiwan. That is too far from Clark for a carrier based aircraft, so we will need to bum an additional ride, perhaps to Jakarta and be picked up there. I will keep on this and let you know. Any reply from Bernie Maroney yet?"

"No, I have not been able to reach him. I will try again this afternoon and let you know."

"Okay. I will work on transport from Clark and will let you know."

"Okay. Thanks."

They hung up.

Lero dialed Bernie Maroney's number again in Jacksonville. It was three in the afternoon in Jacksonville. A sleepy woman answered. Lero identified himself as Dan Roman and asked to speak to him.

"I am sorry, Mr. Roman. Bernie went wild hog hunting in the Dismal Swamp with some of his retired army buddies. He usually turns on his cell phone after dinner in the evenings and most times calls me to check in. I will tell him you called. Is this number a good one to call back on?"

"Yes, ma'am. This is a good number. He can call at any time. I will catch his return call on voice mail if I have the phone turned off. Thank you very much."

"You are welcome, sir. Goodbye."

Lero was just coming in from the back yard barbecue cooker with their salmon filets when the phone rang. He put down the platter and answered.

"Hello."

"Mr. Roman, this is Bernie Maroney, returning your call. How can I help you?"

"Your friend General McKay gave me your name and number. Would you be in a position to put together a squad of a dozen men to undertake a marine operation for me?"

"Probably, but tell me a bit more about what you need," said Maroney.

"It involves air travel to Asia, locating and boarding a ship at sea, without detection, demolition or disabling of some equipment and withdrawal, also without detection."

"How long do you think will be involved, sir?" asked Maroney.

"My best guess right now is somewhere from two weeks to a month door to door."

"Most of my guys are recently retired military. Can I tell them what kind of compensation will be offered and the level of risk?"

"Our assessment of risk is that it would be moderate. Small arms at most. Pursuit at sea, perhaps in a Zodiac, boarding, etc. My people tell me that your people would expect about Thirty Thousand each, in advance. There is a possibility of a bonus if we hit the jackpot. Does that seem reasonable to you, Mr. Maroney?"

"Call me Bernie, please. Yes, that is reasonable. What about equipment and expenses?"

"We have sufficient contacts to supply what we anticipate your people will need. Each man will have expense money to take care of incidentals and we will supply all equipment and expendables (code for ammunition, grenades, chemicals, and other supplies.)."

"This sounds very interesting, Mr. Roman. Since General McKay recommended us to you , we need not discuss any further details about your end at this time. How soon do you need these men ready to travel?"

"We would hope to be able to have them depart for the operation in three days or less. Air travel will be arranged for each man if you will supply the name of the airport they wish to depart from and the names of each operator."

"That sounds fine, sir. I will call you back on this number."

"Thanks, Bernie. I will look forward to meeting you."

Chapter 20

Jean had the cole slaw and sugar free sweet tea waiting. He swung into his seat and they enjoyed a nice meal together. He told her between bites what arrangements had been made.

"When will you go?" she asked.

"Jefe and I will leave in the next three days. We should be gone a couple of weeks. I need you and Ernie to man our headquarters to coordinate things. There is going to be a lot of information flow and we need to make sense of it. It those triggers evade us and get to Disneyland, there could be real trouble. Mr. Murfree involved us personally in this and we need to give him our best effort."

"Will you forget about me on those south sea islands?" she teased.

"I have enough memories of you stored up to keep me occupied for years. Don't worry about a couple of weeks," he said, gripping her hand.

"I am only teasing, but I am concerned about the risk. Will there be armed encounters?"

"We hope not, but any that do occur will be small arms only, we believe."

"Will you be VERY careful?" she asked.

He nodded. They finished their dinner in silence.

"Do you like this new gown," she said, teasingly, as she posed at the foot of the bed.

"I don't know," he said. "I need to examine it more closely."

With that, she slowly peeled it off and tossed it to him.

"That is not what I meant, but it is an ideal response," he said as she crawled up the bed toward him.

Chapter 21

The next morning, just after they arrived at the office, the satellite phone hummed. Lero answered his usual "Hello."

"This is Charles Bostock. Can you talk?"

"Yes, Admiral, thanks for the call."

"I was just calling to confirm that the Reagan is indeed about four hundred miles southwest of Taiwan, but we have a guided missile frigate, the Reuben James, making a port call at Singapore. The plan is for it to be there another four days, then leave for a cruise of the South China Sea and make port in the Philipines in about six weeks. You might want to consider using it if you want to station two teams to increase your chances."

"Wonderful. Thank you, Admiral. How can we contact the Reuben James?"

"I can give you the satellite number of the Combat Information Center officer of the day's desk. Are you ready to copy?"

"Yes sir, go ahead."

The Admiral read off the number to Lero who copied it down and repeated it to the Admiral.

"That is correct."

"Admiral, Jefe and I will be leaving to reposition ourselves in that theatre in the next couple of days. We have a squad of men joining us. If you need to contact me at any time hereafter, you may talk in confidence to Jean, our office manager. She is a member of the unit and has top secret clearance. She will be able to pass messages to us at any time."

"Thanks, Dan. I will do that. Good luck out there. See you later."

"Thanks again, Admiral. Good day."

Lero was about to dial Jefe when he walked in.

"I just talked to Admiral Bostock. We have a guided missile frigate in port at Singapore for the next four days. Why don't we put a team on it and a team on the Reagan to make sure we can board the correct vessel?"

"Now, that sounds like a plan," said Jefe. "Which one do you want?"

"You choose. You have more experience in these matters."

"I will take Singapore and you go to the Reagan. Let's have Maroney split his squad into two squads and get one to Singapore and the other to Clark and the Reagan can send a COD over for us."

"That sounds good. I will call Maroney and see how he is coming along. I can fill him in on the change in plans. He can tell Jean the names and airports of departure and she can get the tickets for all the troops from here."

He turned to Jean and asked, "Can you person this desk for us while we go afield?"

"Sure. It will seem strange without Velma, but I will have her spirit here helping me," she said.

Chapter 22

"Sir, we have found that it is simply impossible to remove all references to our country on and in the triggers. We have removed all insignia from the containers and the external surfaces of the triggers, but if someone disassembles them, they will be able to tell that we made them."

Colonel Pashevsky's comments caused Colonel General Petrof to scowl, even more than his normal facial aspect which was a scowl.

"Very well, Colonel. I know you have done your best. The financial arrangements have been satisfactorily concluded. We consider the triggers now the property of the Islamic Republic. You may withdraw your men and turn over custody to the Iranians. They may sail when they choose."

Pashevsky saluted and said, "I will take care of it, General." He stood back as Pashevsky pushed the button to raise the window of the black Zlin limousine. As soon as the window was closed, it began to slowly roll forward off of the dock and back to his headquarters on the hill above the town.

Pashevsky walked up the gang plank onto the deck and went forward to seek out Major Malik. He found him, standing in the wheel house with the Captain.

"Major Malik. I have been directed to tell you that you are now in control of the containers. You may depart when ready. My men will withdraw and I will signal you from the dock that we have all men ashore." (This was done through the interpreter, who was with Colonel Pashevsky.)

Malik waited for the interpreter to tell him what Pashevsky had said, then brightened, saluted and said, "Very well, Colonel. We will await your signal. Thank you for your hospitality on this short visit."

Pashevsky returned his salute and turned to leave the wheelhouse.

Malik asked the Captain when they could depart. Captain Hordoshoh said that he could depart within the hour, since all hands were on board. He need only call the harbormaster to note the ship's departure.

"Very well, my men are ready. Depart when you are ready."

Chapter 23

George Gordon, the National Security Advisor called Wilma and asked for a time to see the President.

"Is it urgent, Mr. Gordon?" she asked.

"It is not an emergency, but he asked me to come so I need to see him soon, Wilma," he said.

"Come at eleven thirty, then," she said.

"Fine, thanks," he said and hung up.

Gordon showed up promptly and he was ushered into the Oval Office to see the President. He quickly suggested that they take a look at the President's roses, so the President and his National Security Advisor went for a stroll in the Rose Garden. The President motioned him to come closer. He was a bit surprised when the President reached up and pulled his head next to the President's head and whispered in his ear, "George, we have a mole in the White House. I want you to set a trap for him and step up your efforts to sweep the offices and my quarters. Report only to me or Janice. Utmost security. Thanks."

The casual observer would interpret the hug the President gave the National Security Advisor as a friendly expression of gratitude for a job well done under duress. Only the President and he knew what the President had whispered in his ear.

Chapter 24

President Thompson entered the personal quarters a little after noon. Janice was not in the parlor or the bedroom. He was puzzled, but thought she might have stepped out for a moment. He took off his suit coat and hung it on the clothes horse by the bed. As he did, he heard the water running in the bathroom. He tapped on the bathroom door and it opened an inch or two. Steam coursed out near the top of the door and he opened the door wider and spoke to her softly. She was standing in the middle of the bathroom, wearing only a teaspoon of well distributed bath water. She smiled broadly when she saw him and crooked her finger to summon him. He, of course, did not need any encouragement. Janice was a picture of beauty. (She was five seven, weighed one forty soaking wet as she was, and was blessed with a wonderful physique.) Even as wet as she was, he took her into his arms and hugged her. It felt so sensational to him to feel her press against him. She put her arms around his neck and pulled herself up to his ear.

"George found a bug in the residence this morning. I wanted to take all my clothes off to be sure that they were not bugged when I told you. Sorry to be so dramatic about it, though."

He whispered in her ear, "I am glad George found the bug. Thank you for greeting me this way. You can wear this outfit any time you want. Can you stay for a while?" She gave him a soft smile and firmly covered his mouth with hers.

(The next forty five minutes of the President and First Lady's activities will not be reported, since they are not relevant to national security or their official duties.)

When President Thompson returned to the Oval Office, he had a nice glow in his cheeks.

Chapter 25

It was into the third hour of the midnight watch when Tech Sergeant Valerie Griffon pushed the button on the right side of her console to summon the Watch Commander. Captain Evans came down the aisle and stopped at her console.

"What have you got?" he asked.

"Remember, you told us to be on the lookout for a freighter somewhere south west of Vladivostok headed south or west?"

"Yes," he said.

"Well, this freighter is about the same size you gave me and is headed south along the coast of China. There are so many ships in the area, it would be easy to lose it, but the speed you gave us would match with the distance from Vladivostok."

"Watch it closely, Griffon. Report to me at the end of your watch and, at the hand off at the end of your shift, put the next observer on it and tell him or her to keep it in sight."

"Will do, sir."

The second telephone from the right on the shelf above the duty officer rang.

"Major Gurney," was all he said.

"This is Captain Evans at the Overhead Office. Tell your inquirer, that we have a candidate for the ship from Whiskey Thirteen."

"Will do, thanks." The line went dead.

Evans dialed a number and waited.

Chapter 26

Lero's right hand was on Jean's belly, just below her navel. They were sleeping like spoons. The buzz of the satellite phone woke him and he pulled away as gently as he could, but she stirred and rolled over onto her belly as he got up to answer.

"Hello," he said.

"This is Major Evans at Oscar's Place. (This is code for the Overhead Observation platform of the National Reconnaissance Office, headquartered at Dalgren Air Base in Virginia.) What is the password?"

"Ojibwa."

"Sir, we have an observation of a freighter of the size you specified about twelve hundred nautical south west of Whiskey Thirteen, distance fits the cruise speed you gave. We have been tracking for a day. Looks like a definite possibility. What do you want us to do?"

"Stay in contact with it. I will confer with associates to decide on next course of action. Call me with any changes in course or speed, please. Bring me up to date at eleven hundred your time, please."

"Will do, sir. Good evening. Sorry to have awakened you."

"Not to worry. Thanks for your efforts. Appreciate you guys. Good night."

Jean was awake and leaning on one arm when he walked back into the darkened bedroom. The latent light from the sky gave her graceful curves a blue tint. He could not resist hugging her before he spoke.

"They have a ship sighted that is the right size and direction and distance from port. They will update us at eight our time. By the way, how did you get to be so beautiful in this light?"

"A dark haired stranger showed me how. I was never beautiful before he came into my life."

She rolled over against him and they both gave a prayer of thanksgiving as they snuggled and tried to go back to sleep.

Chapter 27

Jefe felt strange in two ways as he came into the converted Quonset hut where they had their headquarters. He missed seeing Velma at her desk. She had been part of his life for twenty five years and he had loved her like a brother loves a sister. No one could ever replace Velma personally, but Jean was up to the job professionally and had a vast storehouse of skills that Velma had not had. Velma had her own different skills and had been a priceless asset to the unit. The other pang that hit him was that he was no longer in charge of the unit. That passed quickly as he appreciated how well and smoothly Lero had slipped into the commander's chair and assumed command of the unit, and how much he and Alita were enjoying his retirement. Lero and Jefe worked seamlessly together, as if they had been together for decades and were meant for working together.

Jean was at the desk on the telephone when he came in, so he just waved and smiled at her. Lero could see Jefe through his office door and motioned him in. Jefe sat his coffee cup on the desk and took a seat before he spoke.

"Doesn't seem the same without Velma," he said.

"I don't think it will ever be the same, but we will carry on. I miss her, too. But, Jean is doing fine. She is so scary smart, that she will have this place by the handle any time now."

It was a couple of minutes before eleven. Lero called to Jean to come in to the office. She was a picture of office efficiency in her dark blue polka dotted dress and heels. He thought to himself that she would be a picture in anything or nothing.

"I want you both to be here when they update us from the Overhead office. I asked them to call at eleven."

Jean took a seat beside Jefe.

Lero said, "They called me from the Overhead office last night about four. They have spotted a suspect freighter the right distance from Whiskey Thirteen and along the coast, south bound. I had the fellows from Janes send us photos of the two suspect freighters so we could study their structure to be sure of the identification."

He put the photos on the desk in front of them. Jefe picked up one photo and the large magnifying glass with one smooth motion. Jean picked up another photo and began studying it.

"How are we going to make sure of the identity of the ship?" she asked.

"That is what we are here to decide," Lero said.

"What are our available options?" he asked, looking at Jefe.

"Well, most ships have large numbers on their decks or forecastles for use in overhead identification. If this ship has those numbers, we can identify it by satellite or overflight."

As Lero was about to pose another question, the telephone rang. He hit the speaker button, picked it up and answered, "Hello."

"This is Major Dudding at Oscar's place. Say the word, please."

"Ojibwa," said Lero in reply.

"Sir, we continue to track that freighter for you. It is now about one hundred nautical east of Taipei, still steaming at twelve knots. Do you want us to continue surveillance?"

"Yes, thank you, Major Dudding. Give me another report in about eight hours, please."

"Will do, Sir. Good day."

They sat silently for a few moments, each with his and her own thoughts. Then Jefe spoke, "What is your plan?"

"I talked with Bernie Maroney at Fayetteville. He is putting together a squad of recently retired operators. I think I would place one team of six on the carrier in the South China Sea and another at Singapore, in case we fail to accomplish what we intend with the first team. I want you to go with the team to Singapore. Jean will stay here to coordinate our efforts and I will go out to the carrier with Bernie. We will coordinate with him to plan a boarding or something else. We can stay in touch by satellite phones. At the rate the ship is steaming, he is making about two hundred fifty nautical miles a day. That means, roughly, we have five or six days to catch the freighter in the South China Sea and your team will have about twelve days before it gets to Singapore and enters the Malacca Straits. We each need to spend some time with our operators to show them how to disable the devices and avoid detection. We need to get Ernie to come from Tempe to schoolhouse us so we know what we are talking about."

Chapter 28

(In Russian)

"Gorky, I want you to be careful with the crew. They drink too much vodka. I am afraid their safety procedures are weak. Can you cut back on their daily ration a bit?" asked Captain Zenoviev.

"I will do my best, Captain, but these guys are soaked and stay drunk while at sea to make the time pass more quickly."

As Gorky left the bridge, he passed the cook, Nickolai Kamanyev, bringing the Captain his mid-morning coffee.

"Ah, Kamanyev, thank you for the coffee. Nice day, isn't it?"

"Yes, Captain," answered Kamanyev, and looking around and seeing that they were alone, asked "You don't think anyone suspects me, do you, after the last minute substitution of me as cook?"

"Not these guys, Nickolai. The aggregate intelligence quotient of the whole crew is probably less than one hundred. These guys are vodka soaked long time sailors and they do their jobs and sleep and that is about it."

"I need to make my daily security inspection of the cargo, Captain. When can you go with me to do that?"

"I can go in about twenty minutes, when the first mate takes over the wheelhouse. I will meet you in the forward companion way forward of the hatch into the hold."

"Very good, Captain."

After the first mate took over, Captain Zinoviev went down into the companionway as agreed and found Kamanyev waiting at the hatch. The hatch was chained with a lock on the chain. Each man had a key to the lock and they unlocked the chain and opened the hatch and went in. Both had flashlights and lit their way over to the wooden boxes on the port side. Kamanyev looked all around each case and determined that there had been no tampering with any of them. He nodded to Zinoviev and they both went back out of the hold and secured the lock. Kamanyev then went back to his galley and the Captain went to his compartment for a nap. The old freighter lumbered on into the afternoon.

Chapter 29

Jean stood to go back to the outer office, but hesitated and asked them, "Did you know that Velma kept two handguns in her desk?"

"Yes," said Jefe. "I bought her the Smith and Wesson Airweight several years ago as a Christmas present. She carried it in her purse. The Ruger LC9 was bought in the last five years for her to keep in her desk, just in case. I think they should be yours now, Jean."

Jean hesitated for a moment, then said, "Thank you. I will take good care of them."

She turned and walked back to the outer office to her desk. She took out the Airweight, checked that it was loaded, and slipped it into her purse.

Chapter 30

Captain Fulweider responded to the intercom from his station at the head of the array. Seaman Dresser had pushed the button on his console that made a yellow button light up on Fulweider's console. Fulweider pushed his chair back and walked over to Dresser's station about half way back in the AWACs fuselage.

"What do you have?" Fulweider asked.

"Captain, I have been watching this freighter for a while, as you ordered. It is still making about twelve knots and has changed course to about a heading of two zero five. But that is not why I buzzed you. Look here, about a thousand yards behind the freighter. This shadow looks like a submarine. Why do you suppose a submarine would be tailing this freighter?"

"I don't know, Dresser, but I will report it. Take a shot of what you are seeing and send it to my computer, and keep watching. Report any changes. Good work."

"Thanks, Captain. Will do."

As soon as he received the photo, Major Askanazi printed a copy for desk use and reached for his magnifying glass. He got out his calipers from the case in the desk drawer, too. After he spent some time examining the shadow behind the freighter, he called the Ops Center.

"Ops Center, Major Brady."

"This is Major Askanazi of overhead analysis office, calling from Alpha Nineteen. I need to speak to Admiral Cushing."

"Just a moment, hold one."

After just a brief pause, the phone was answered, "Admiral Cushing's office, Commander Blake."

"Commander, this is Major Askanazi from the overhead analysis office, presently in AWACs Alpha Nineteen. I need to speak to Admiral Cushing."

"Just a moment, Major."

"This is Admiral Cushing, Major. What can I do for you?"

"Admiral, we have been tailing that freighter per your orders. It is now about three hundred miles south of Taipei on a heading of two zero five, still making about twelve knots. We have noticed that it is being tailed by a submarine. Our analysts believe that, based on the length of the sub and the shape of the nose and tail, that it is a Russian diesel powered Attack Sub."

"Thank you, Major. That is good work. Send the picture to my email, please, and maintain surveillance."

"Will do, sir. Thank you very much. Good day."

"Good day, Major, thanks again."

Jean was typing a report when the phone rang. She answered as she usually did, with just "Hello."

"This is Admiral Cushing at the Overhead Department. Say the word, please.

Jean said, "Klondike."

"Thank you. Our analysts believe that the freighter you have had us watching is being tailed by a Russian Attack sub. I am sending Lero an email with a picture."

"Thank you, Admiral. I am sure he will be grateful for the information. Do you want him to return your call?"

"That is not necessary. Give him my best regards and he can call if he needs to."

"Thanks again, Admiral. Good day."

"Good day."

Chapter 31

When Jefe returned home about three in the afternoon. The Altima was in the garage and he pulled in beside it. Alita was not in the kitchen or the living room, so he looked out the kitchen window and noticed that the gate to the pool area was ajar, so he strode out. She heard the gate squeak as he opened it, and looked up. She was near the end of her sunbath and was covered with her favorite French suntan lotion and nothing else.

"What a nice surprise," she said. "Is everything OK?"

"Oh, sure," he said. "I had a nice visit with Jean and Lero at the office. Something has come up and I need to travel a bit. I may be gone a couple of weeks. I would invite you to go with me if I felt it were a safe place for you to see the sights, but it is Singapore and I would be uneasy about you being out alone. I think it is better that you stay here. Jean will be staying here, too and you two can visit and shop together."

"Is Lero going, too?" she asked.

"Yes, but he will not be with me. He will be somewhat to the east from me, but we will be in constant touch."

She got up from her air mattress and walked over toward him to retrieve her serape and floppy hat. He was every bit as speechless as usual as he watched her walk toward him in the afternoon sunlight. Her tan was not interrupted by bathing suit marks and she was a remarkable sight.

"You must come in and help me get this suntan lotion off," she said, giving him a nice kiss, but not touching him anywhere else for fear of staining his Palm Beach suit.

As he opened the gate for her, he said, "I am so glad we got you a good supply of that French suntan lotion. It tastes as good as it smells. I love you in coconut."

She gave his hand a warm squeeze.

Lero was at the shooting range when Jean buzzed him on his phone. He did not answer right away, but noticed the message when he had finished a string of .45 slow fire at fifty yards, and returned her call.

"You have a message from Eagle Eye," she said.

"Oh, good. I am just finishing up. I will be there in ten minutes."

"Okay. See you then."

Lero brought his gun box into the office rather than leave it in the car where the ammunition would get too hot.

He sat it down next to Jean's desk and gave her a little smooch.

"I like having you here with me. Being able to give you a little kiss and a hug and a pat makes the day so much more pleasant. What did the Admiral send?"

Jean took the photo out of the desk drawer and handed it to Lero. He studied it for about half a minute and looked up at her and said, "Wow. Those guys are good. Do you know what this is?"

"Admiral Cushing said it was a Russian Attack Submarine."

"I need to make Bernie Maroney aware of this. It may affect the choice of help he is putting together."

"I will get you his number," she said.

Chapter 32

The barracks smelled of tobacco smoke, sweat and spilled alcoholic beverages. Yuri Petcovich stepped into the darkened hall from the bright light outside and it took him a bit for his eyes to adjust to the dimmer light. The coal stove in the middle of the squad bay was doing its best, but the corners of the room were still chilly. The commandant's room door was ajar. He tapped on the door and was greeted with "Come in."

When Captain Isamov looked up and saw who was entering, he jerked up from the side of the bed and did his best to come to attention without falling headfirst onto the hardwood floor. The man who stood in the doorway did not wear a military uniform, but instead simply had an enameled badge in his suit coat lapel button hole. Isamov recognized it immediately as identifying the wearer as a member of the Federal Security Service, the successor to the KGB.

"At ease, Captain," said Petcovich. "I did not mean to startle you. I just need to speak to you confidentially."

"Sorry, sir. I was not expecting your visit. How shall I address you?"

"My name is Yuri Petcovich. You may call me Mr. Petcovich."

"What can I do for you, sir?"

"Please have a seat," said Petcovich.

Isamov sat down again on the bedside, still in his pajamas.

"I am here to change your orders for your next voyage. Your written orders, which have been placed in the safe in your cabin on the submarine, will remain the orders that any inspector might see if he examined them. However, I am giving you some special orders, orally. You will not tell your crew anything other than that the cruise is a special training exercise. We estimate that the cruise will take ten weeks and you may put into port on the way back from your journey to give the men shore leave in Jakarta or Singapore, as you choose."

Petcovich swept aside the glasses and plates on the table in the middle of the room and unrolled a chart on the table. Isamov stepped over to be able to see what Petcovich was telling him.

"You will sail from Vladivostok on Tuesday. Your mission is to leave shortly after and shadow and safeguard this ship, the "November Victory" and make sure that it is not tampered with or boarded on its journey. It will be sailing on Tuesday also and its destination is Bandar Abbas in Iran. You will proceed underwater behind the November Victory and so as not to be observed by it. You may surface at night to recharge your batteries. We have chosen you and your attack submarine because it has tactical weapons rather than the atomic submarines which only contain nuclear torpedoes and intercontinental ballistic missiles and because your boat can cruise unobtrusively on the surface and submerged to periscope depth using its snorkel at the same speed as the November Victory. For once, it seems to have been a good strategy to have kept these ancient rust buckets in commission. Now your ship's unique features will fit the mission we have planned very well. Your updated electronics bay will enable you to observe the November Victory from a suitable distance. You may need to surface to repel boarding parties if some foreign government has detected what we are transporting and tries to interfere. You will have twelve crew members on this cruise who are trained commandoes who will augment your regular crew. They will have their own arms and equipment to enable them to maneuver on the surface and take appropriate action if the need arises. In case of an unfortunate event, they will be most useful. With conventional 533 millimeter torpedoes, a one hundred millimeter deck gun, a forty five millimeter antiaircraft cannon and a Dushka machine gun on the conning tower, you will have sufficient tactical capacity to repel any boarding party. If you encounter a military ship that attempts to seize the November Victory, you are to sink the November Victory immediately, and note her position's latitude and longitude. You will not pick up survivors unless there are no other ships in the area. There are three containers of classified material on board in wooden crates about three meters long and almost a meter square on the ends. Once the ship makes port, you will lay offshore and observe the unloading as best you can. Once the containers are unloaded at Bandar Abbas, or whatever other port the ship puts into, you will proceed back to Vladivostok, with the port call along the way. We have arranged for a tanker to be in position to refuel you. On your way back, a tanker will meet you west of India. They will broadcast their position on the frequency noted in your sailing orders to guide you to them. You will not broadcast to anyone unless you are in distress and need to abandon the mission. Once you have turned for home with your mission accomplished, you will broadcast the phrase, "Happy Day," in English one time at or near two thousand hours that day. Have I made myself clear, so far?"

"Yes, Mr. Petcovich," said the astonished Isamov.

"One more thing, Captain Isamov. You may instruct your second in command to visit your safe and open the envelope marked with the letters S-17, if, for any reason, you become incapacitated, Therein he will find instructions to complete the mission. Any questions?"

"No, Mr. Petcovich, thank you for the honor of this mission. We will be ready and will sail as you direct."

"Very good, Captain. You should know that Admiral Strelnikoff chose you personally for this mission from a list of candidates. Good performance on this mission will assure your consideration for future assignments," said Petcovich, who then turned and left quietly. Isamov sat on the edge of the bed and briefly contemplated the burden of the mission before him, then reached for his underwear and began dressing himself.

His breath steamed at Captain Isamov addressed the crew on the dock next to Submarine bC-43. All eighty six men stood at attention. Captain Isamov informed them that they were going on a special training mission to assess the capability of the ancient submarine in today's electronic warfare world. He told them that they would be gone about eighty days, that they would run submerged most days and surface only at night, but that when the mission was completed, they would have a port call at a welcome tropical port.

"We are all volunteers. Let us show them our best. That is all."

With a nod to the First Officer, Captain Isamov turned command over to him and the First Officer began giving orders to assign tasks to the deck crew and others to get ready to get under way. No one on shore waved or smiled as the submarine cleared the breakwater and made for the open ocean. In half an hour, the boat was out of sight.

Captain Isamov made a log entry: "15 Sep 2015: Departed V at 1833 hours, with eighty six crew, full fuel tanks and a full complement of stores."

Once they got clear of shore, the captain ordered the Navigator to set a heading of one fifty five degrees for the first three hours, and to advise the radar and sonar operators and lookouts to look for the November Victory and close with it. The captain ordered that he be informed at the first radar or sonar contact. The old sub hummed along, making eighteen knots, as darkness fell.

Chapter 33

Lero dialed his regular cell phone. In a few seconds, it connected and began to ring. "Hello," was the only greeting.

"Bernie, this is Lero. Call me back on a secure phone. Thanks."

"Will do," said Bernie and hung up.

Lero knew that it would take Bernie some time to get to a secure phone, so he busied himself reading the latest intercepts and overhead data on his secure email site.

There was a nice clear picture of the November Victory, still steaming south-southwesterly and a dark shadow about fifteen hundred yards behind. The analysis from the Overhead guys said that, based on the length and the bow shape, the submarine was thought to be a diesel type, first commissioned in the fifties, when the Russians, then the Soviets, were still using engine designs acquired from the Germans. Lero remembered when he and Jean had toured the German Submarine 515 at the Naval Museum on the Chicago lakeshore. He had been very impressed with the quality of the workmanship and the efficacy of the design.

"Why would the Russkies use an ancient sub like this on such a mission?"

Perhaps Jefe could answer the question, he thought as Jefe entered the outer office.

Jefe spoke to Jean and they both came into the inner office and sat down at Lero's desk. Lero showed them the picture and the analysis, and asked Jefe why he thought the Russkies would use such an old sub for the assignment.

"I can think of one reason in particular," said Jefe. "Their nuclear subs do not have any tactical weapons, like a deck gun or machine guns. In my opinion, this sub is much better qualified to tail the November Victory. If they need to take action against a boarding party or shipboard interference, this sub is much better suited."

"I called Bernie and asked him to call me on a secure phone. I want to bring him up to date with this development," Lero said.

"Alita is busy packing. She is so excited to be included in one of my business trips. I am so glad I changed my mind about taking her with me. Thank you for agreeing to let me take her. We are staying at the Hyatt Americana in Singapore and I asked for an upper floor to get the view and the better security. Thank goodness for our encrypted phones, otherwise, I would be very concerned about cell phone security."

"When do you leave?" asked Jean.

"We will leave Sky Harbor at nine fifteen tomorrow morning. We go from there to Narita. We will have most of a day there, then leave on a Cathay Pacific flight to Singapore. My old friend Wesley Richards from the British foreign service has made a nice warehouse available for our team to assemble and prepare. The quartermaster can deliver stores and equipment there before we get there and Wesley is providing security around the clock. How do you want me to handle the financial part of this with Wesley?" he asked.

"You can take some blank checks for the larger amounts, if you want, and enough cash for contingencies, but you can use your charge card, too, for the convenience. It was nice of our friend to provide the charge cards this time. A professional touch," said Lero.

"I have made up a list of code words for this mission. Jean can keep hers handy here, but it would be better if you and I memorize the names and not take this list with us," he added.

Jefe nodded his agreement and took the three by five card that Lero handed him.

"Be careful out there, Harry," said Lero as he and Jefe rose to leave.

They looked at each other directly for a moment then shook hands. Jefe smiled at them both as he turned to leave.

Jean went back out to the main office and followed Jefe to the door. After he left, she locked the front door and returned to the inner office. Lero was once again examining the picture of the November Victory with the submarine tailing it, so he did not see her unbutton her dark blue polka dot dress and slip it off. She came to the other side of his desk and, standing there in her tan pumps and nothing else, said to him is a conspiratorial tone, "You were in such a hurry to get here this morning, you forgot to take care of something."

He looked up, noticed that she was in his favorite outfit, and blushed beet red. Quickly regaining his composure and sense of humor, he said, "You are so beautiful. How could I have been so forgetful?" as he started around the desk toward her. He decided to give her a nice hug and a kiss and hold her hips in his hands before he went to the closet for the air mattress. As he did, she went over and turned off the lights.

Chapter 34

Later that morning, Lero was back at his desk when the secure phone rang. It was Ernie calling from Tempe.

"Good morning," he said. "Say the word."

Lero said, "Houston. What is the good word?"

"Calistoga," was Ernie's reply.

"What is up," asked Lero, now that the parties were sure they were speaking to the intended party.

"I have some data on that fish you asked about."

"Pray tell," said Lero.

"We believe it is what NATO classifies as a Foxtrot class boat. Diesel electric, project 641, probably built in the sixties. Upfitted with late model electronic gear, though. They built seventy five of these boats, but there are only six known to still be in service. Most of the Russian sub fleet is rusting in the harbor at Polyarny."

"Thanks, Ernie. Once we found out about the fish, we knew that we would have to change our approach plans. If you would keep an eye peeled for any intel from Fort Huachuca about activities in the South China Sea, it could prove helpful. I will be changing locations tomorrow or the next day and Jean can advise you when I get there where I am. Our soccer team is suiting up and will be enroute in the next few days."

"Good, I will keep in touch and you do the same."

"Thanks, Ernie. Appreciate your help."

"Just be careful out there."

"Okay. Bye."

"Bye."

(Note to the technically inclined: Fort Hauchuca is located about fifteen miles north of the Mexican border, about forty miles west of Tucson. It has a long and distinguished record among the Army and the Air Force, though very few civilians even know it exists. Now manned by a complement of eighteen thousand troops, it is home to the Network Enterprise Command (NETCOM) and the U. S. Army Intelligence Center. It was the fort in the late eighteen hundreds from which the U. S. Cavalry battled Geronimo and the Chiracahua Apaches. Presently, the Advanced Airlift Tactics Training Center calls it home and the fort maintains a large aerostat at fourteen thousand feet MSL to provide radar coverage and other surveillance of the Mexican border as well as provide a station for numerous specially tuned antennae for sigint and elint interception.)

At lunch at the Sonic, in their white Grand Cherokee, Jean told Lero how grateful she was that Jefe had installed a full bathroom with nice fixtures and a shower in the office building. "Do you suppose that Jefe and Alita have used it like we do?' she asked, snuggling against him.

"I have a high degree of confidence that they have. We never have talked about such things, though. Jefe has had to spend long hours at the office and during stressful times, has camped out there for several days without leaving. I would hope that Alita would have brought him meals and a massage during those stressful times, wouldn't you?" he asked.

As he turned to her to get her answer to his question, he met her mouth with his. It was a deluxe lunch.

Chapter 35

When Jefe and Alita arrived at Sky Harbor Airport, it was just a bit after eight. They walked to the Northwest counter and Jefe rolled their carry-on bags. The bigger baggage had been checked at the taxi stand outside the terminal. The 747 upon which they would fly was nosed up to the terminal by the windows of the waiting area. Jefe told her that the plane had so much fuel on board that the vertical stabilizer had a fuel tank in it. The flight to Narita would be fourteen hours plus. Both Jefe and Alita are avid readers, so each had a couple of books to read on the way and Jefe had some "technical journals" that he planned to study, too.

The plane departed on time, with Alita and Jefe in the first class compartment on the second level. The runway run was longer than Jefe thought it would be, but the outside temperature was over ninety and the density altitude was way up that morning. By the time the plane got a couple of hundred feet above the runway and began tucking its eighteen wheels into their wells, he could feel the reassuring climb pressures of a normal 747 departure. The flight attendants served an elegant lunch as they passed over San Diego outbound.

"Harry, there is one tiny thing that concerns me about traveling like this."

"What is it, my dear?" he asked.

"Well, since I probably won't be able to sunbathe like we usually do, my tan will fade and I am afraid you won't find me as attractive." She gave him a wicked smirk.

"That is something that you need not concern yourself about, Alita. There will never be enough of you. However, if it is secure enough, I will ask the Concierge if you can sunbathe in the altogether at the rooftop pool."

"You are so thoughtful, Harry. Will you put some suntan oil on me before you go off to do whatever it is that you are going to do in Singapore?"

"I promise," he said to her and gave her a kiss at the base of her neck.

When they arrived in Narita, after reading most of the way and three terrific meals, they went to the Cathay Pacific desk to pre-register. The nice lady with the melt in your mouth English accent, gave them passes to the Club, so they could rest up for the next flight and watch the television to get current with world events if they wanted to, and otherwise enjoy the finest hospitality any airline can provide. The Club had subdued lighting so people could snooze in the recliners if they chose. They could watch TV with ear phones to keep the noise down and enjoy the finest cuisine anywhere or a nice cold beverage. They appreciated the ambience of the Club, but both decided that they needed to take a walk since they had basically been sitting for fourteen hours plus. The assured the attendant that they would be back shortly and embarked down the concourse. Like most upscale international airports, there were first rate merchants and restaurants where they walked.

By the time they had walked about a quarter mile, they began to look for a restaurant. A nice looking Oriental restaurant beckoned, so they went in and had a sumptuous meal of steamed crab, fried rice and white wine. The marvels of international jet travel had deposited them in Narita in the middle of the afternoon and they had been up for almost twenty four hours. When they got back to the Cathay Club, they slept for hours in adjoining recliners in a secluded corner.

The news on the television droned on about elections, tragedies, terrorist bombings, international monetary strife and the like, but they slept through it all.

Fortuitously, they both awakened about an hour before the first call for passengers for their flight to Singapore. They adjourned to their separate wash rooms to freshen up. They thanked the kind and dignified ladies of the Club for their hospitality and Jefe left a nice gratuity in the wine snifter on the desk by the door.

As they walked back up the concourse, the silver tongued lady with a perfect Oxfordian accent on the public address system announced that Cathay Pacific flight twenty for Singapore and Delhi would be boarding at gate C-9 in approximately forty minutes.

Chapter 36

Admiral Strelnikoff was reading the morning dispatches and drinking his morning coffee from one of those clear glass cups the Russians favor, when Captain Pugachov arrived. He did not get up, but waved Pugachov in.

As usual, Pugachov stopped in front of the desk and came to attention and saluted Admiral Strelnikoff, then brought his leather dispatch case around the huge desk so he and the General could go over the contents he had brought.

The first item was a satellite photograph of the South China Sea. A small dot on the photograph was the November Victory, he told Strelnikoff. The subtle shadow about fifteen hundred meters to the rear was the bC-43, he said.

"All seems to be in order. The freighter is making normal progress and there has been no indication of detection or interference," said Pugachov.

"Good, good," said Strelnikoff. "Glad things are going according to plan. What I really want to hear is the situation in Ukraine and Chechnya."

"Very well, Admiral. The troops we have sent there in neutral uniforms continue to entrench themselves in the countryside of eastern Ukraine. Ships arrive daily to disgorge equipment and supplies for the effort. No one seems intent on restraining our progress and we should soon be at a strength level where we can begin our westward progress. The Air Forces has have been busy reading the satellite photographs to make up targeting lists for our bombers and our missile submarines."

"Good, Alexi. Anything else to report?"

"Yes, Admiral. I regret to inform you that there has been a problem at the Naval Base at Sevastopol. Several sailors over indulged in alcohol and staged a mutinous riot. About forty men were involved. The military police had to use deadly force to put an end to it and there were several casualties. Only one military police person was wounded, though. The public relations officers have taken care to compartment the whole episode and those who might report untoward matters have been reassigned and admonished to keep quiet about the episode. We believe the whole thing may blow over without any reports in western journals."

"That is too bad, Alexi. What do the intelligence people say caused the situation?"

"It was alleged that the cause was non-payment of a month's wages, the working conditions and discipline and an overabundance of vodka, sir."

"Sooner or later, our higher ups are going to realize that the conditions of the men and the junior officer corps are dismal. Sevastopol used to be such a nice place to be stationed."

"Yes, sir," said Pugachov. "Things have changed from the old days. Then, it was a prestigious thing to be a Naval officer or sailor. Uniforms were neat, food was readily available and our men were treated well by the local population, but lately, with the shortages, the townspeople are envious of our men's food supply and their vodka rations. The bars and taverns are not nearly as happy as they were ten years ago. The local prostitutes have mostly gone elsewhere because the sailors have no ready cash when they come ashore."

"Ah, yes, Alexi. I remember what a welcoming place Sevastopol was when I was a junior officer. The girls were pretty and clean and friendly. There are fond memories of such things in this old sailor's mind. Let's see what we can do to facilitate more prompt payment of the men, especially those coming ashore from lengthy cruises. It would improve morale tremendously and improve local public relations, too."

"Should we consult your adjutant to prepare an encouraging letter, sir?"

"That would be a good idea, Alexi. Bring me a draft copy when you can."

"Very well, Admiral. Is there anything else just now?"

"No, Alexi. Thank you for the briefing."

Captain Pugachov gathered up his papers and photos and stuffed them into his dispatch case, then went around to the front of the desk, came to attention, saluted and turned on his heel on the deep wool plush carpet. Strelnikoff turned to the frost covered window for a peek at the square. It was a dark afternoon and looked like snow.

Chapter 37

The satellite phone buzzed on Lero's desk. He reached for it and pressed the send button.

"Hello," he said.

"This is Bernie, calling on a secure line," came the reply.

"Hey, Bernie, glad to hear from you. What is your twenty?"

"I am in the office of the commandant of the Intel Unit at Fort Bragg. Colonel Shaffer is an old friend and former commanding officer."

"Are you alone?" asked Lero.

"Yes, sir, I am," said Bernie. "I am calling to report that I have twelve men ready to move. I would recommend that you disburse the advance to my account and let me send each man his advance. I can email or fax the routing numbers and the account numbers."

"Okay, that sounds good. I will send you a wire transfer. Please add an estimate of the travel expenses to get the men to Vandenberg. I would like to have a team meeting on Thursday about eighteen hundred hours. If you will fax me their names, I will arrange gate passes and the guard will have a pouch with directions for each man so they can find the Visiting Officer's Quarters and the meeting room."

"Will do, sir."

"Thanks, Bernie. See you Thursday."

Lero then called the Base Commander's office at Vandenberg. When he was connected to the Base Commander's office, the phone was answered by Major Cartright.

"Major Cartright, this is Lero, L-E-R-O, calling from Davis Monthan. We plan to have a team of twelve operators arrive at your base on Thursday for two overnights at your Visiting Officer's Quarters. I will need visitor's passes for them and a meeting room of appropriate size from eighteen hundred hours to twenty hundred on Thursday. We will depart by arranged transport sometime on Friday. The authorization code is Turkey Hunt."

"Very well, Lero. Message received and understood. If you will fax the names to me at 716 888-9543, I will have the passes ready and the reservations at the Visiting Officer's Quarters. We will expect you and your men on Thursday. Travel safely and call this number if you need anything further."

"Thank you, Major Cartright. See you Thursday."

Lero dialed another number. "Pacific Command Ops Center, Captain Mallory speaking."

"Captain Mallory, this is Lero. L-E-R-O. I need rapid transport for thirteen men on Thursday or Friday from Vandenberg to Clark. Would you check and see what is available and call me back? The authorization code is Turkey Hunt."

"Thank you, Lero. Message received and understood. I, or my counterpart, will call you back with an availability."

"Thank you, Captain Mallory. Good day."

Next Lero dialed a familiar number.

"Pacific Fleet, Ops Center, Commander Blake speaking,"came the answer.

"Commander Blake, this is Lero. L-E-R-O. I will need transport from Clark to the Reagan sometime Saturday or Sunday, seven troops with equipment. I also want you to alert the Reagan that we will be boarding and that we will be conducting special ops from the Reagan in the days following our arrival. You may call this number twenty four seven to respond."

"Thank you, Lero. Message received and understood. I will call you back when the arrangements are in place."

"Very good, Commander Blake. Thank you. Good day."

"Good day, sir." The line went quiet.

Lero went to the large storage closet adjacent to his office and picked out a rucksack and began putting items into it for the trip. His combat boots, several pairs of camouflage trousers and tunics, his night vision goggles, K-bar knife and scabbard, pharmaceutical pouch, first aid kit, a couple of MREs, his binoculars, his shoulder mount combat radio transceiver, forehead mounted flashlight, a quick erecting floating folding radar reflector, swimming mask and flippers, wet suit, scuba tanks, a one man rescue inflatable raft, his EPIRB (Emergency Personal International Radio Beacon), the Browning Hi-Power nine millimeter pistol he usually carried on black ops, a bandolier of ammunition, his Heckler and Koch nine millimeter fully automatic close quarters assault weapon, several boxes of energy bars and a six pack of sports drink. By now the ruck weighed over sixty pounds and he pulled it out into the office beside his desk to await the placement of more items in it. He sat back down at his desk and took the fax from Bernie and made out a wire transfer request for enough to cover the anticipated travel expenses and the advance payment for each man. When it was complete, he faxed it to Banc Suisse in Geneva.

Later that afternoon, Captain Mallory called from Vandenberg.

"Sir, I wanted to get back to you regarding your request for transport. We don't have anything from here going near Clark on Thursday or Friday, but I found that there is a B-1 leaving Travis for Diego Garcia on Thursday that could drop your guys off at Clark. Would that be okay?"

"That would be just fine, Captain Mallory. Do you have a contact at Travis for me so I can make arrangements for gate passes and Visiting Officer's Quarters reservations and facilities?"

"Sure. Call Major Burnham at 617 543-8976. Good luck, Lero."

"Thank you, sir. Good day."

Next, he called to see if there were a local flight going to San Francisco on Thursday. The sergeant said he would call back with an availability.

Things were beginning to come together.

Chapter 38

At eighteen hundred two hours, Lero stepped into Room 108 in Building 45 in the Intelligence Battalion of Travis Air Force Base. As soon as he opened the door twelve men got quickly to their feet as he walked to the front of the group. He put them at ease and they sat again.

"My name is Lero. L-E-R-O. I want to thank each of you for undertaking this assignment for us. If you have a cell phone, put it on the table in front of you, please. We will collect them and return them to you after this briefing."

Now, I want to meet each of you individually," he said and moved forward to shake hands with each man.

"Blankenship, sir, Newport News, Retired Seal."

"Good to meet you. Thanks for coming."

Each man gave his name and home town and a brief bio. Lero returned to the front and they sat.

He continued as the corpsman picked up the phones and put them in a cardboard box and left the room with them.

"Your presence tells me that you are satisfied with the financial arrangements and that you are willing to at least hear what this event is all about. Since each of you has a security clearance, we will be able to share certain details with you that we would not be able to share with your regular service colleagues. Bernie tells me that seven of you men are recently retired Seals and the rest are from the Special Operations Battalion at Fort Bragg. I want you to divide yourselves into two teams of six. You are much more able to make a good division of your ranks than I am. You will need to do that before you leave here, which I estimate will be Thursday morning. In order to help you decide on who will be on which team, let me give you an outline of the mission."

"Last Tuesday, eight days ago, a ship left a Russian port and is now in the South China Sea. Our information is that it is headed for a port near the Straits of Hormuz. There are three items on board that are being transported to Iran, which in our unit, we refer to as Disneyland. You may use either name, however."

"Your mission is to board that ship, put one of us in a position to alter the items and depart the ship without detection. If we are detected, we will need to use lethal force and possibly take other action. You need to keep in mind that this cargo is so important that a submarine is tailing the ship and any boarding and shipboard activities will need to be such as not to alert the submarine. What we are asking you to do is within your training and expertise. We will provide whatever transportation you decide upon to put you in a position to execute. We also want you to divide into two teams so we can take two swings at this apple if we need to. One group of you will go to Singapore and will be under the supervision of my associate, Jefe. He will coordinate your transportation and will be responsible for providing you with the equipment and stores that you want. Jefe is the recently retired chief of our unit and has a long and distinguished career in the area of special operations. I want you to keep in mind as he watches out for you, in certain ways, that I want you to watch out for him, too. Jefe is sixty four years old and in good shape for a man his age, but he is no match for you guys. He can find and provide any piece of hardware or service you might need. The man has friends all over the globe who have worked for him and with him for a number of years."

"While you are considering the mission as far as boarding and leaving the ship, I want you to become familiar with what you are going to encounter. We are all adults here, gentlemen. This is serious business. We want you to disable or sabotage three nuclear bomb triggers."

There was complete silence as he resumed.

"At this time, I want to introduce Dr. Ernie Galvin, who will address some particular technical facets of your mission. I need to tell you that he is also retired Admiral Galvin, who was commandant of the Special Warfare Detachment at Dalgren Naval Base before his retirement. He is familiar with all the nuclear devices in service in all the countries of the world who have such weapons. He is now and has been for a number of years, Professor of Astrophysics at the University of Arizona at Tempe. His expertise is deep and preeminent. Having thoroughly embarrassed him, I am sure, I will cease all that and just introduce Ernie Galvin."

"Good evening, gentlemen. Lero was too kind in his introduction, but let's begin. The devices we are going to disable are Russian, manufactured approximately eight years ago, which places them in what we call the Seventh Generation. Nuclear devices have evolved generationally. Sometimes a trigger will be improved while the explosive device will be the same as the generation before and vice versa, sometimes the device will be improved and the trigger will stay the same. So we attach a Generation number to each. At present, we believe that the Russians have approximately fifteen thousand nuclear devices. The type that we are concerned with here are Generation Seven, which implies an equivalency to twenty thousand tons of TNT, roughly two times the power of the device that destroyed Nagasaki."

"On the screen here, you see an example of the trigger portion of the Gen 7 nuclear device. This trigger is capable of detonating devices in the range of twenty thousand tons of TNT down to five thousand tons. We believe that the devices you will encounter will look exactly like the one pictured here. Notice the numerous panels that are affixed to the body of the trigger. These need to be removed by backing out the countersunk Phillips head screws. The choice of panel is critical here. If you remove the wrong panel, you will not be able to access the part of the device we want you to work on. If you count panels from this main circumferential ridge three forward and four down from the eye bolt at the top that is used the lift the device with a crane, you will have the correct panel. Remove it and expose these eight wires. We believe that the best way to sabotage this device in the haste that we find ourselves is to substitute three of the wires for wires that contain no electrode. They will probably detect this rather quickly, but we want you also to substitute this computer card here (pointing with a laser light pointer) and plug in a bogus card that we will supply you with. If they power up the device with the substituted card in place, it will destroy all the software that causes the device to follow the detonation protocol, which means, in plain English, that it will make the device a complete dud. Since time is one of our enemies here, we want you to substitute the card so that they will have transported the devices all the way to Iran and to their secret facilities and checked it over before they power it up. The longer we can extend the discovery period, the more difficult and time consuming will be the effort to repair or replace the devices. We foresee and hope that the Iranians will suspect that the Russians have gamed them and sold them a set of devices that the Russians know are defective. This, we hope, will cast a shadow of doubt over the parties as far as trust is concerned for future negotiations, in addition to delaying their testing of the nuclear devices that would be detonated by these triggers."

"It is going to take us a couple of days to get your teams into position. Military hardware will be involved. I am leaving ships diagrams and photos of the type of ship we are going to board. We have arranged transport to the south Pacific that will depart tomorrow afternoon. I will remain behind and will be available to answer questions at any time, night or day. I will be camping out in my office for the two days that we anticipate you will be at the critical stage of this mission, so you can reach me. I will supply numbers and frequencies to your team leaders who can give it to you."

"What we want you to do is to devise a plan to get yourselves onto that ship, disable the triggers and leave without a trace. Let's meet again tomorrow about ten hundred and go over your plans and put this thing together."

"You can stay in this secure room as long as you want. You can order any food you want from the Sergeant or go to the mess hall. Stay as late as you want. Discuss this among yourselves here and elsewhere, but be careful whom you talk to after you leave here. If anyone tries to engage you in conversation, please report that to Lero immediately. His cell number is on the board there. Talk to each other guardedly and only when you are relatively certain you are not being overheard."

"Thanks for undertaking this mission. We will meet again tomorrow morning."

Lero and Ernie then left the meeting and the fellows to let them put the assault plan together.

Chapter 39

Jefe and Alita stepped off of the Boeing 777 that had brought them from Narita into the steam heat of Singapore. As they went through the customs area, Wesley Richards stepped out of the crowd and greeted Jefe warmly. It had been many years since they had seen each other even though they communicated often by phone, email and fax.

"Well, how are you, my fine friend. You don't look a day over seventy."

"Nor do you, you old walrus. Glad to see you have taken good care of yourself and not gotten old and fat. I want you to meet Alita Goodman, that we have spoken about."

"Yes," he said, doffing his white straw hat. "I have heard so many nice things about you. Welcome to Singapore."

"Thank you, "said Alita. "Harry has told me many complimentary things about you, too. Nice to meet you, too, finally."

Wesley reached over with his left hand and handed her a green felt bag and told her to slip it into her purse.

"This is for your protection here in Singapore. We have a very effective police department, but they cannot be everywhere and a well-dressed westerner may prove to be more temptation than thieves can resist."

When they got into the taxi, Alita examined the bag and found a loaded Ruger LCP .380 caliber automatic. Since it was the same type weapon Jefe had given her some time ago, she was familiar and grateful for the security it afforded.

Wesley had the driver gather their baggage and take them on a round-about tour of Singapore before taking them to their hotel. The circular driveway in the front of the hotel contained several luxury cars and taxis as they arrived. Since Wesley was a familiar personage at the hotel because of the number of people he brought there, and because he was a good tipper, the porters scrambled to the bags as soon as he was seen getting out of the taxi.

Wesley stayed with them as they registered and went up with them to their rooms to make sure that the rooms were suitable and to chat some more with both of them.

"I will bring Brianna back for dinner at seven if that is okay. She wants to see you both, too, and we can have a nice dinner here at the hotel."

"That would be delightful, Wesley. You will be our guests. Thank you for your guidance today and your hospitality. See you at seven," said Jefe.

After Wesley left, after tipping the porter who brought up the bags, Alita went to the French doors that opened onto a terrace that overlooked the city.

"Isn't it lovely?" she asked. "Thank you so much for bringing me with you. This is terrific."

"Yes, it is lovely, indeed. I am so glad you came. It is so nice to have you with me."

"A long flight like that, always makes me want to shower and change."

"Me, too. I will help you. I need a shower, too."

"Harry, you are so considerate," she said as she wrapped her arms around his neck and kissed him ardently.

The telephone rang with a message from Wesley. "Meet us at the Golden Dragon Restaurant at seven. Taxicab driver will know directions. See you then."

As they stepped from the cab in front of the restaurant, an oriental man stepped up and hissed, "Give me your money, old man," and flashed a knife with a long shiny blade. Jefe instinctively reached back with his right arm to move Alita behind him and obediently reached for his wallet with the other arm. Just as he got his hand on his wallet, keeping his gaze intently on the robber, there was a flash of light and a sharp noise to his right. The robber staggered as if struck by a large object and crumpled to the brick street. Jefe turned to his right and saw that Alita had reached past him on his right side and fired a well-aimed shot at the robber. Jefe's mouth was wide open in surprise.

When he regained his composure enough to speak, he said, "Thank you. Are you okay?" in respectful astonishment.

"It was a reflex action. I have never had to shoot anyone before. Oh, Harry. Now, I am so scared."

"It's all right. You are safe and I am, too, thanks to your quick action. Let's let you sit down while the police arrive."

The taxi driver who had seen the robber approach them and heard the shot, came around quickly and said, "Most sorry, sir. Robbers like this are everywhere. I call police," and he scurried around to his radio and did so. It seemed like only minute before they heard the siren of a police car that arrived just a few seconds later.

By this time, the robber had lost consciousness and lay on his back with the knife next to his hand. There were two officers in the car. One went to the robber immediately and felt for a pulse. He took out his cell phone and called. Then he used the cell phone to take several pictures of the robber from various angles. The other officer came to them and asked, "Are you okay? Are you hurt?"

They both assured the officer that they were unharmed, but shaken up.

He said, "Once the ambulance arrives, my partner will accompany the suspect to the hospital and you can come with me to make a report. I need to ask you for your firearm, too."

Alita handed him her purse and the officer removed the Ruger and placed it in an evidence envelope, being careful not to smear any fingerprints.

By now the full gravity of what had happened hit both Jefe and Alita and they were glad to be able to sit in the police car to compose themselves. Alita leaned over onto Jefe's shoulder and sobbed.

"Oh, I hope I have not killed him," she sobbed.

"If he is dead, it is his own fault," said Jefe. "Thank you for saving our lives, Alita. That was a very brave and resourceful thing to do."

"I am so glad you took the time and care to train me. Wesley must have remembered that you gave me a Ruger just like this one for Christmas last year. It felt so familiar."

She clung to him as they rode to the police station. By the time they got there, Wesley was there to meet them. He showed his diplomatic credentials to the officer after which the officer took a recorded statement from them both. Then the officer returned the Ruger to Wesley and told them that he would be back in touch if he needed further information. Jefe told the officer that they were staying at the Hyatt Americana, and they were allowed to leave.

Chapter 40

"The way we see it," said Bernie, "the best way to assault the freighter is to parachute down in front of it and using one man rafts, get ourselves into its path and using hooks on poles to catch the lip of the gunwales of the deck, boarding as quietly as we can. With the load we think she is carrying, the lip of the deck will be about sixteen feet above water, not too far to reach with our poles and hooks. The ambient noise level in these old freighters is high enough that we think we can release an anesthetic gas into the air intakes for the compartments below decks to disable the crew and for the bridge, too, without detection, which will give us more time and leeway to alter the triggers and get away without detection. A normal crew for this ship would be twelve to fifteen men. If we hit them in the middle of the night, say one thirty to two thirty, we think we will have our best chance, with the fewest number awake. A plane at altitude will not attract any suspicion, we think. They could not hear it anyway, with the ambient noise on a freighter this size. With six guys parachuting in a spaced array, we stand a good chance of getting two or three or maybe more onto the freighter. If we get close enough, we can paddle close enough to get us into the path of the oncoming freighter and allow us to board. Being out front of the freighter keeps us out of sight of the submarine, too. If we land too far to paddle, we could use small outboard motors to get close. Once the mission is accomplished, those who succeed in boarding the freighter can link up, and those who don't make it aboard can be separately ex-filtrated, once the submarine has passed. We have the architect's drawings for the sister ship of the November Victory, so we can study how to assault if necessary and how to enter the holds without detection. We will need some special equipment, but it should not be difficult to obtain, fabricate or transport it. We made a list of what we know now that we will want. Perhaps it would be better to try to obtain it stateside and take it with us rather than scrounge it up out in the Pacific theatre."

"Do you have the list?" asked Lero.

"Sure, said Bernie and handed it to Lero.

"Let's see, fifteen one man inflatable rafts, fifteen five horsepower outboard motors, paddles and plugs to seal holes, fifteen five gallon tanks with fuel, fifteen suppressed automatic assault rifles, preferably not US made, and preferably nine millimeter. with five hundred rounds for each man, semi-automatic handguns for each man, also nine millimeter, fifteen tanks of anesthetic gas and valve mechanisms, wet suits and flippers for everyone, radar reflectors for everyone, MREs and a sports drink supply for everyone, enough for six days at sea, in case we have difficulty getting spotted and picked up, black suits for us all, camouflage fatigues, too, wrist compasses for each man, and EPIRB for each man, black square Mark Eleven parachutes, boarding party issue combat knives, first aid kits for each man, a large combat first aid kit for the unit's use, night vision goggles, shoulder mount radios, an aircraft band transceiver for each man, flashlights with infrared filters, infrared strobes, goggles with infrared filters, duct tape and plastic tie wraps to secure prisoners, if any, night visible wristwatches for us and altimeters we can read on the way down, shark repellant, dye markers, flares for each raft, four one-pound charges of Semtex for each man, with timer detonators, any gear you think we need to breach the containers and change the wires and circuit boards, and a rabbit's foot for luck."

(NOTE: An EPIRB is an Emergency Position Indicating Radio Beacon which broadcasts a signal that is picked up by stationary satellites.)

When Lero read the last item, the group enjoyed a laugh.

"What if you and your men are detected and the whole thing goes wrong?" asked Lero.

"If we have to kill or imprison the crew, we will have plenty of time to disable the triggers and maybe engineer a boarding by a friendly nation to throw off suspicion."

Ernie and Lero nodded their agreements.

"I will arrange transport for our team, Bernie. Pick which team you want to go with me and we will send the other team to Singapore."

"Sir, we anticipate that if we have to take a second swing at the apple, it will be much more difficult to board in stealth. We anticipate a more forceful approach."

"I agree," said Ernie. "If we have to try a second time, we may lose the advantage of stealth and may have to take more aggressive steps. There will be a lot of traffic at the inlet to the Malacca Straits, though and we can conceal our approach on the surface much better. But, letting the cat out of the bag may cost us the desired result. Destruction of the triggers may be the only viable alternative to disabling them, as you planned."

"Alright, Bernie, have the guys choose teams and appoint a team leader for the team going to Singapore. Let Ernie and me know what the call signs will be for each team and each man. I will meet everyone at the ready room at the airport at twelve hundred hours. Our transport is expected then."

Lero let the men go out, get some sleep and relax a bit before the flight. He dialed his cell phone. It was answered at the Quartermaster's Warehouse by Sergeant Peterson.

"Sergeant Peterson, this is Lero – L –E—R—O, my authority is Turkey Hunt. The unit number is forty seven. I am at Building 45. I need some equipment and stores delivered to the ready room at the flight line before eleven hundred this morning. Can you send a man over to pick up the list? This is a quiet request, Sergeant."

"I understand, sir. Someone will come over and pick up your list right away."

Chapter 41

The Captain came into the conning tower just before sunset. The first officer was scanning the area surrounding bC-43 from periscope depth.

"Just coming to relieve you, Boris," said the Captain.

"Very good, sir. No traffic sighted except our freighter. Seas are relatively calm, with only two foot swells."

"Very well, I relieve you."

"I stand relieved," said the first officer and saluted.

"Get some rest. We will surface in about half an hour to charge batteries and let the men go up on deck if they want. The outside temperature is twenty five degrees." (He means Celsius, which is about seventy seven degrees Fahrenheit.)

The night was soft and overcast, with a scattered ceiling of shallow clouds at about four thousand feet above sea level. The bC-43 made the same twelve knots on the surface as submerged, to keep up with the freighter. No running lights were displayed contrary to international norms, but this was a secret mission. The Captain admonished the lookouts to be extra vigilant for shipping other than the November Victory. All motored along calmly.

Chapter 42

Lero arrived at the ready room an hour before the appointed time. He wanted to make sure that things were in order before the group departed. About ten minutes after he arrived, a six by six cargo truck pulled up to the gate and was buzzed onto the tarmac. A sergeant got out of the right seat and came in to the ready room with a clip board.

When he stepped in, seeing that Lero was the only person in the room, he cautiously asked, "Sir, does your name start with 'L'?"

Lero said, "Yes, I am Lero. Are you from the Quartermaster's office?"

"Yes, sir. Sergeant Graves. We have your shipment, in containers ready to load for you."

"Fine, Sergeant. If you and your men would wait here, our transport is expected any time. We would appreciate it if you would help us load."

"Will do, sir. Would you sign the receipt, please?"

Lero signed the lengthy receipt and gave the clip board back to Sergeant Graves.

"I will wait with my men in the truck, sir. Let me know which plane is yours and we will load your equipment."

"Thanks again. You guys are tops."

Graves smiled in appreciation and turned away to walk back to his truck.

The first of the men arrived at the ready room. Benny Hudnall was a stocky Marine. He had qualified as a SEAL after several years in the service, and had recently retired to the Tidewater area of Virginia. He carried only a small bag of necessities for the trip.

Shortly, the other men began arriving and within thirty minutes, they were all assembled and ready to go.

An airman tapped on the door frame and said, "Sir, your aircraft has called in and is on final approach."

"Thank you, airman," said Lero and the men all looked out toward the runway to watch it land. One of the things Lero had learned about the B-1 is that, on landing, they need to let the brakes cool before taxiing to the ramp, so he told the guys why there was a delay. It was a rush for them all to see the swing wing bomber approach and flare to land. It taxied in and shut down. The crew de-planed after a couple of minutes and walked into the ready room.

Major Jenkinjones led the six man crew into the ready room. Lero came over to them and introduced himself and let the groups mingle and introduce themselves to each other.

"Since we have been detailed for this trip, I need to visit the flight planning office to file a black flight plan. It won't take me long, maybe half an hour. You and your men are welcome to check the loading of your cargo and board, if you want. My men will help if need be, and will give you and your men an orientation of the plane."

The outfitters had installed two double rows of nice comfortable seats in the open area behind the flight deck. The crew explained that, due to the length of the flight and the concern that any contingency be anticipated and provided for, there would be two complete crews on board. That way, they could switch off and some could rest during the flight. The cabin crew members, who were not pilots, explained that there would be at least one aerial refueling and there might be a second if the winds aloft were not beneficial. Since the flight would be direct and take about seven hours, there was plenty of food and drink loaded aboard, too. They explained that the commercial airliners took about twice the time to make the same flight, but that they would spend almost all of their flight time once they got over the ocean at high cruise speed. They explained that regulations required that they maintain less than Mach 1 over the continental United States due to noise concerns. From Travis, they would be over the ocean in a matter of just a few minutes, they explained.

In a few minutes. Major Jenkinjones and his co-pilot reappeared. He took a minute to brief the passengers on the flight and then they adjourned to the flight deck. Lero and his men strapped in for takeoff. In a few minutes, the bomber came alive and the engine noise became obvious. With a small lurch, the brakes released and they taxied to the active runway. Lero felt the big plane turn onto the active runway and, after a short pause, it powered up and they all were plastered into their seats by the acceleration. He was always amazed at the rush of power. True to prediction, they were over the ocean in less than ten minutes as they climbed into the blue. Lero thought he felt a burble when they went trans-sonic as they climbed through flight level three zero zero. He wondered how Jean was.

Chapter 43

Alita came out of the bathroom in a short champagne colored satin gown. Jefe had had the steward put their meal on the table that was covered with a linen table cloth. He could not help himself and stared at her as she ambled toward him. She was a picture of loveliness. She caused a tensing in his stomach every time she did that, even after all the years that they had known each other. She slid into the chair he held for her. He kissed her neck and lower down her front as far as he could nuzzle his nose before the gown made it impossible to go further.

"You are so good to me," she said.

"I was going to say the same thing to you," he said. He loved the memory of how soft her breasts were against his mouth.

"I am so glad you ordered in tonight. We need some time to unjangle, don't we?"

"Yes, we have had quite enough outside influence for today. I just want us to have a nice, quiet meal alone and go to bed early."

"Are you sleepy, Harry?" she asked.

"Not in the slightest," he said.

"You say the nicest things," she said, as she put her linen napkin on her bare legs.

They ate the magnificent the seafood feast that he had ordered, gratefully. After dinner, they sat on the sofa and watched the news on TV for a short while. She slipped off her gown before she snuggled with him.

Chapter 44

Walter Baines asked the President's Secretary for a brief appointment. "I just need a couple of minutes of his time, Charlotte," he had said. Baines had become Deputy National Security Advisor to the President when Howard Carmichael had been diagnosed with cancer and had retired.

Later that day, Charlotte buzzed Baines back. "He can see you at four fifteen. Is that okay?"

"Yes, Charlotte, that is fine. Thanks."

At four ten, Baines dutifully reported to Charlotte. He took a seat opposite her desk to wait his chance to see the President.

Just a few minutes later, the intercom buzzed and Charlotte nodded to Baines. He rose and went to the Oval Office Door. The President was standing in the conference area beside one of the sofas.

As Baines approached to shake hands with President Thompson, he gestured to indicate that he wanted to talk to the President outside in the Rose Garden. They walked out of the President's office and down the stairs to the Rose Garden.

"I am betting that you did not request this tour of the Rose Garden to examine my fine Helen Traubel roses, Walt," the President said in a low voice.

"That's right, sir. I have a list of suspects and I want to try something to see if my theory is valid."

"What do you want to do, Walt?" asked the President.

"We will put around the clock surveillance and electronic surveillance on the suspects and we will give each of them a piece of information that they alone will have. If we detect a sniff of the secret information being transmitted, we will either be able to nail the mole or go to the next level of surveillance. If we are lucky, we will nail the mole on the first go around, though."

"Do you have a list of suspects with you, Walt?"

"Yes, sir. Take a look. I want to take the list back once you have read it, though."

"Fine," said President Thompson and scowled at the list Baines handed him.

There were five names, all employees in the upper levels of personnel in the White House.

"Sir, we plan to place a bogus message with a key word or phrase or number in information normally handled by these suspects. Each one will get a different message, so we can tell which one is our mole if that information is transmitted by radio, paper, verbally, text, or e-mail. We would rather you not know what the key words are."

"That is fine with me, Walt. This is most distressing. I will help you any way I can. Tell me what you need me to know as this progresses. Thank you for doing this for me. It really bothers me that someone we trust is selling us out."

"Okay, Mr. President. I will give the go ahead to our team."

The President asked, "What if one of them sends an encrypted message? How will you detect the presence of the key word or phrase?"

"Mr. President, I cannot discuss that here, even with you, sir."

The President was a bit taken aback, but attributed Baines' caution to the fact that they were talking in the open in the rose garden where it was remotely possible that their conversation might be overheard by sophisticated means.

Baines sensed the President's puzzlement, but said only, "I will let you know what happens."

Baines turned and went back through the Oval Office and the President took a short stroll through his Rose Garden. His Secret Service detail of two men watched closely from behind the pillars.

Chapter 45

Sergeant Knowles unstrapped and came back to the seats where Lero and his crew sat. Because of the high ambient noise, Lero and his crew were wearing earplugs. When he saw that Knowles wanted to speak he took out his earplugs and Knowles said, in a loud voice, "Major Jenkinjones says that we will be descending and slowing down shortly to refuel. Our approximate position is three hundred nautical south of Midway. This will take about twenty minutes. Then we will climb back to our cruising altitude. We still expect to arrive at Clark in another four hours."

Lero said, "Thanks, Sergeant," and the loadmaster went back to his seat and strapped in. In a minute or two, the plane began to decelerate. The noise level dropped and they could feel the deck tilt downwards at the front. There was only one small window on each side of the B-1 and they took turns watching the wings swing forward from full back position to a more straight out sweep. One of the guys said that he could see that they put on a bit of flaps to slow down. The refueling itself, after the B-1 connected to the drogue on the KC-10, only took about eight minutes. Then, they felt the bomber descend a bit and turn to the right. In a minute or so, they felt the power come back up and the plane began to climb and accelerate. The guys settled in for another four hours. Some read and some slept and some just dreamed while awake.

Their arrival at Clark was smooth and uneventful. The pilot flying made a nice landing and they rolled to taxi speed before they turned off the runway.

Sergeant Knowles came back and said, "There will be a truck alongside in a minute to take your luggage and gear to your temporary quarters. I have been in the Air Force for eighteen years and I think I can see a special op in the works. I know you guys cannot talk business, but I just wanted to wish you a safe journey."

All of Lero's men shook hands with Knowles as they deplaned and thanked him.

Lero saw to it that his men and their luggage and equipment were unloaded from the B-1. He thanks Major Jenkinjones and his co-pilot, Murphy, for a safe and quick trip. After Jenkinjones and Murphy departed to sign post flight reports and go to the Visiting Officer's Quarters, Lero found a private room. He took out his satellite phone and called a familiar number.

"Ops Center, Pacific Command, Major Hardy speaking."

"Major Hardy, this is Lero, L-E-R-O, authority is Turkey Hunt , Unit forty seven, we have arrived safely at Alpha Three and will need transport for a unit of six operators and equipment from Clark to the Carrier Reagan. My men need rest, so we would appreciate it if we could depart Clark in approximately twelve hours."

"Right, Lero. I will inquire and report to you on this number. Good Evening."

Lero went back to the squad bay to talk with his men. Bernie and the guys were gathering their gear and luggage. A driver had brought a small bus over to take the men to the transient crew barracks.

As Lero walked up, Bernie and the men turned to him to listen.

"Men, get some rest and chow. Sleep if you can. We will meet here at zero nine hundred in the morning and I will lay out the rest of the mission for your comments and input. Thanks, guys."

They nodded to indicate they had heard and understood what he said and they filed out to the bus.

The sergeant at the Transient Crew Quarters greeted them warmly. He assigned rooms to the men in pairs and Lero got a room to himself. They unpacked, then came back to the front office to get directions to the chow hall.

Fortunately, the chow hall was just down the block from the Transient Crew Quarters and the men immediately decided to walk over. It was nice to get some exercise and fresh air after the long flight and inactivity. The men arrived at the chow hall with renewed vigor and enthusiasm.

The steward asked Lero to sign for the meals for himself and his men, which he did. The men filed in and got trays to fill with their dinner. Typical of operators, they knew that the local personnel would recognize them as outsiders and they were not upset by that. They smiled at the servers and took their trays to a table out of the main stream of diners. They ate quietly and eagerly. It had been a long time since the men had had a good meal. The smell of the food and the bread was enticing and they all appreciated a good meal. Conversation was light and trivial, with nothing of substance discussed. These men knew their jobs and understood security.

After a fine meal, the men strode leisurely back to the Transient Crew Quarters and went to their several rooms. It wasn't difficult at all for the men to get some sleep.

Chapter 46

Jean opened the dryer door and scooped out the clothes she had put in before. As she filled her arms with dried clothes, the short silver gown that she and Lero like so much, fell across her arm. She looked at it and gently pulled it from the other garments and carefully hung it on a cloth covered hanger and hooked the hangar on the wall. She spent a few moments just looking at the gown and thought about the times she had happily worn it and gleefully removed it. She remembered how dear the times were when she and Lero had lounged and slept with her wearing that gown. She remembered at times waking up in the morning to find the gown across the sheet she slept under and how dear those times were when she reached for Lero and found him close by. She took a moment to say a prayer to protect Lero and his men as they went in harm's way, far from her laundry room in Tucson. She hugged herself and looked up at the ceiling and she dreamed of their special times together.

Chapter 47

At about three forty five in the morning, the Desk Sergeant tapped on the door of Lero's room. Since it was a secure facility, the doors were not locked in the Transient Crew Quarters, he opened the door a couple of inches and spoke to Lero, "Sir, are you awake?"

"Yes," said Lero, "I am awake. What is it?"

Your man, Smithson, has taken ill. We have summoned an ambulance to take him to the hospital on the base. We cannot tell if it is food poisoning or perhaps an appendicitis attack."

"I will come right away," said Lero.

By the time he got to the lobby, the paramedics were wheeling Smithson out on a stretcher. His face was white and sweaty, but as they wheeled him past Lero, he reached up and took Lero's hand. "I'm sorry to let you down, sir."

Lero bent over him and said, "Not to worry, Smithson. This is no one's fault. Take good care of yourself and we will visit with you at the hospital. Thank you for your service."

Lero and the remaining five members of the team gave each other questioning looks and shook their heads at the unfortunate turn of event. They filed back to their rooms and tried to get some sleep as they wondered about the welfare of their teammate. It took all of them quite a while to get back to sleep.

In the morning, Lero showered and went to the lobby to walk over to the Mess Hall. Two other operators arrived at the same time, so the three of them walked over and had a grand breakfast. As they ate, Lero's phone rang.

"Hello," said Lero.

"Sir, this is Major Hartung at the Base Hospital. We had to perform an emergency appendectomy on your man Smithson. He is resting comfortably and will need to stay with us for a few days. Will you take care of notifying his family? We have no information about him in our database."

"Yes, Major Hartung. I will notify his family. Thank you and your staff for your quick and professional response. We anticipate leaving your base shortly. Please tell Smithson when he is out of sedation that we will let him know how things go. Tell him also that he has our well wishes and prayers for a full and speedy recovery."

"I will do that, sir. Good day."

After he got back to his room, Lero dialed his satellite phone. Jefe answered on the third ring. After they exchanged coded passwords, Jefe asked, "What's up?"

Lero said, "Our man Smithson has had emergency appendicitis surgery in the India Four hospital. Please notify his family that he is okay and will be coming home in a few days."

"Will do. How does this change your plans? Do you want me to send a man to replace Smithson?"

"No, that would take too long. We are expecting transport in the next couple of hours to the intermediate location we discussed. I will be inserting with the men in Smithson's place."

"Respectfully, do you feel up to that? You and I are no longer spring chickens, you know. How long since you made a HALO jump?"

(NOTE: A HALO jump is a parachute descent from high altitude with low opening. It is used to assault in secret and is usually carried out at night.)

"Thanks for your concern, but I am in good shape for this. The last HALO jump I made was two years ago over Disneyland from the Nighthawk. I am in the right frame of mind to do this and the men are a great team and I feel we really need six men to make our odds better that we will succeed."

"I will need to get Jean to contact Smithson's family. Should I tell her that you are going in with the team?"

"I will leave that to your discretion. She would probably want to know. Do we have a ship tailing the freighter and the sub?"

"Yes, at our request, Uncle has dispatched a guided missile frigate that is transitioning from station in the South China Sea to Newport News for six months to follow the freighter and sub at a cautious distance. It is in place."

"Okay. We will wait to hear from you before we plan a second attempt. The men are here and in secure quarters waiting for the go ahead. Our information is that the boat will reach the Straits of Malacca sometime early next week. Right now, it is about three hundred nautical south of Taipei."

"Okay, thanks. I will be back in touch after we have our crack at this."

"Be careful out there."

"I will. Thanks. See you later."

The line went silent.

Chapter 48

Lero had reserved a conference room for nine hundred hours and the men assembled.

He told the men that Smithson had had a successful appendectomy and was recovering nicely. He thanked the men for their quick handling of Smithson's illness. Then, he rolled out a chart showing the inner structures of a sister ship of the November Victory.

"I am grateful that you men undertook this mission for us. I have read each of your files and I am impressed that you have the experience and skills to get this done for us. What we are going to do is hitch a ride on a Carrier Onboard Delivery aircraft in a while which will take us to the USS Reagan, from which we will deploy at the best time to intercept the November Victory. Our plan is to place a team of operators above the November Victory and parachute into the sea in front of the ship, swim over into its oncoming path, use boarding pole hooks to climb aboard and then disable the triggers in the hold. If we succeed, we will withdraw before anyone discovers our presence or what we have done. I will arrange for a ship to tail the November Victory at a discreet distance and await an opportunity to pick us up. I think it is a reach to think that we all can snag the ship and board her. Some of us will probably miss the chance either due to not being close enough in front of the ship to get to it and board, and some of us may land in the sea behind the November Victory and miss the chance. In either case, we are determined to try to disable these triggers as we have been tasked to do. Do any of you have any suggestions or observations?"

"Sir, how will we get from the Reagan to the position over the ship? Will we need oxygen?"

"I think we will use another Carrier Onboard Delivery aircraft, so we will have the speed, range and lifting capacity to take our team aloft. Yes, we will need oxygen. We will bail out at high altitude, so as to pass overhead with a minimum sound signature and will be doing so in the middle of the night. Our weather reports that there will be light winds in the area due to a large well developed high pressure area. We will be parachuting in wet suits and under black canopies. We will take enough inflatable rafts to serve the entire group, and enough weapons and ammunition."

"Will five of us be enough, sir," asked Marsden.

"We think we should deploy every available man, so I will go with you," said Lero.

There was a silent pause.

"Who will be in charge, sir?" asked Fazio.

"Bernie will be in charge of all tactical maneuvers. I will be in charge of logistical and communications needs. I will contact our support personnel when we are ready to be ex-filtrated. I will try my best to stay out of your way and let you get this job done, but there might be a situation where I could contribute to the mission. I feel responsible to send a team of six as planned."

"Okay," said Bernie, "then it is decided. When do we leave?"

" A COD from the Reagan will pick us up in an hour. Let's get our gear and go out to the flight line to wait for our ride. Thanks, guys," said Lero. He rolled up his chart and they filed out.

In due time, the COD landed at Clark Air Base and taxied to the flight office. The pilots shut down and, after a moment or two to post flight the aircraft, deplaned and walked into the flight line office.

Lero stepped over to the door and greeted the pilots as they entered. He introduced himself and got the names of the pilots and then introduced the pilots to the group.

"We just need to take a pee break and we will be ready to take you to the Reagan, guys," said Lieutenant Corder. "You can stow your gear and equipment in the aircraft as soon as they finish refueling. Will you get your loadmaster to report the weights to me, so I can do a weight and balance calculation before we depart?"

"Sure, Lieutenant," said Bernie.

In twenty minutes, the pilots and Lero's crew gathered beside the aircraft. Bernie handed Corder the weight report from the loadmaster.

"It looks to me like we will be taking off near maximum permissible gross weight. The flight to the Bush will burn off about half of our fuel, so we can land on the Bush at a good weight. For those of you who have never landed on a carrier, I need to tell you that when we land, you need to have your seat belt tight, since we will be brought to a stop with the arresting gear cables on the deck of the carrier. This aircraft will weigh about the same as a fully fueled and bombed up F-18 Hornet. We will be brought to a stop in about two hundred feet, so it is a jolt if you are not ready. Flight time is about an hour and twenty minutes. If you are ready, let's go."

The men filed into the aircraft, each strapping in to his seat. The left engine began to moan and then whine as it came up to operating speed. The pilot released the brakes after the second engine came up and they taxied out to the active runway. In a few minutes, they were on their way.

The pilot made a short field take off, lowering the flaps to full at about forty knots. At sixty knots, the COD lifted off the runway and the pilot held the nose level with the runway to build up airspeed, then he climbed away as the milked the flaps back to a normal position for climb out. As a pilot himself, Lero was impressed with the smoothness.

It was a beautiful daytime flight from Clark to the Reagan. They approached the carrier just at dusk, so they got to see the carrier below as the pilot flew a normal approach pattern. As the pilot began his final approach, he came on the speaker and told everyone to be sure to pull their seat belt tight. The touchdown was a bit rougher than a commercial flight, but immediately after that, they were decelerated abruptly. Lero's seat belt bit into his belly as his body was tossed forward in the seat. He was glad to have braced his torso by putting his hands against the seat in front of him.

The carrier had looked so small and so short below them as they approached it. The grey ship in the dark blue water was so small, it seemed. Now, as the COD turned to taxi back to the elevator to be lowered to the hangar deck, the deck seemed so big. The pilot stopped the COD near the tower and cut the engines. Deck hands swarmed the plane to post-flight it. The door was opened and they all went out to get their gear. Lero and the guys thanked the pilots for a smooth flight and, in five minutes, the COD was being towed to the elevator.

Lero and his men followed a crewman to their quarters. When they reached the bay where they were to bunk, a Lieutenant welcomed them and gave each of them a lanyard with a plastic card on it that identified them as a VISITOR. He gave them a chart with directions to the head and the chow hall and the crew recreation room where they might watch television or a movie using the CD player.   He told Lero that the Captain would send a seaman later to bring him to the Combat Information Center. The guys settled in to rest before chow.

Their gear and rucksacks had arrived by a different route and arrived in the companionway on a wheeled cart. Each man retrieved his rucksack and the crewman took the rest of the gear to a storage room nearby.

Chapter 49

Captain Bingham was a bit heavier than Lero expected, but he received Lero with a welcoming smile and handshake.

"Our orders are to place you over the November Victory at night for a HALO drop. My feeling is that it will be better if we use the COD to take you there without getting the ship too close. We are now about three hundred nautical from the freighter. My suggestion is that you get your guys ready for a drop tomorrow night. We can have the COD ready to depart with you, say at zero one hundred hours or so, and let you out over the freighter about zero two thirty local time. Do you think your men will be rested up enough to keep that schedule?"

"Sure, Captain," said Lero. "My guys are champing at the bit already. They will be good to go as you propose."

"Good. Well, I will probably be back in touch if anything changes. Be careful out there."

"Thanks, Captain. See you later," said Lero and followed the seaman back to their quarters.

A night catapult shot from an aircraft carrier is a unique experience. For a passenger, it is a jarring start to a flight into the blackness. Lero and his men gathered in the Ready Room, all jocked up and with their rucksacks filled with inflatables and gear. They put their rucks into a cart brought in by a seaman, who trucked them out to the elevator and took them up to the flight deck where loadmasters put them into the COD. It was black dark, with a thin overcast and stars above. Lero addressed the men: "Most of you have done this several times before. A night HALO jump into the ocean is familiar territory for you. Try to stay together as much as possible once out of the plane. May the Lord bless you and keep you. Thank you for doing this for our country."

They went out in a line and they were so bulky with equipment that they needed to send only three up on the elevator at a time. As they stepped out onto the flight deck, the noise level rose considerably. Wind across the deck was about thirty miles per hour, thanks to the combination of the prevailing wind and the speed of the ship through the night. Their flight would be the first of the evening and as soon as the pilots saw Lero and his men emerge from the hatch in the side of the tower, they called the Flight Boss for permission to start engines. As the men filed into the COD, Lieutenant Justice started the port engine, number one. It moaned and groaned, then whined and then screamed as it came up to the power producing range.

Lights blinked, rotated and flashed on the deck, on the aircraft and in the hands of the deck hands as they guided the pilot over to the catapult. As the COD lined up, a flight deck hand fastened the catapult yoke to the nose gear. Now the pilots did their final pre-takeoff check list.

Brogan keyed the mike for the speaker in the passenger compartment and said, "Okay, fellows, here we go. Get a good grip."

Lero and his men hunkered in the seats, held onto their knees and waited for the jolt. Lieutenant Brogan called the flight boss, the equivalent of the tower at a land based airport.

"Flight Boss, six three four is ready to go on the right."

"Six three four, you are cleared for cat shot. Contact departure on two five niner decimal seven. Have a good flight."

"Six three four, roger. Good evening."

Brogan and Justice pulled their yokes full back, gave the deck boss a snappy salute, then put their helmets back against the head rests and waited. The deck boss knelt and put his left hand on the deck. The catapult operator, watching through a thick glass window about fifty feet forward saw the signal, paused a moment to check for a clear deck one last time and mashed the large green button to his left. In less than a second, pressure came up in the catapult, the mechanism tautened and the forty thousand pound COD was hurled forward down the deck and into the night.

After they realized that the cat shot had gone well and they were on their way, Lero and his men relaxed a bit and shuffled around in their seats to achieve some comfort as they climbed into the night. In ten minutes, the pilot flying (Brogan, in this case), leveled the COD off at flight level two zero zero (twenty thousand feet above mean sea level) and trimmed for cruise flight, bringing the power back to cruise setting from climb power. Wind noise built up as the COD transitioned to cruise speed.

Chapter 50

An hour later, as they drew near the estimated position of the November Victory, Justice turned the radar antenna twenty degrees down to look for the ship.

"Volcano, six three four."

Six three four, Volcano. Go ahead."

"Give us a vector, please to jackpot." (NOTE: Six Three Four has its transponder switched off. The satellite tracking 634 is reading a primary return only.)

"Overhead guys advise jackpot is eighty clicks (kilometers) at your one o'clock."

Brogan clicked his mike key twice to acknowledge the information. The less said on the air, at this time, the better. Brogan pushed a rocker switch to light the red light in the passenger compartment to alert Lero that they would be bailing out in less than five minutes. The men checked their gear one last time and shuffled around in the passenger compartment and got into a string in the area between the seats. Each man behind the first man took hold of a loop on the parachute harness of the man in front of him. Together, they shuffled toward the door at the right rear of the compartment.

The pilot had slowed the plane to loiter speed to reduce its noise signature on the sea's surface and to let the guys bail out with minimum turbulence when they hit the slip stream. Still, it was about one hundred ten miles per hour. Just before they were to bail out, the pilot lowered the landing gear and the flaps and brought the speed down to about eighty five miles per hour. They were at twenty thousand feet over the surface of the South China Sea. The outside temperature was right at freezing. He gave them the green light signal and they piled out the door as quickly as they could. The closer they were when they left the aircraft, the closer they could land in the sea. Lero was the fourth one out. The cold air hit him like a slap, but he righted himself and held his arms against his sides to descend at maximum speed. His wet suit protected him from the blast of the cold air, but there were places where the air penetrated between wrapped layers of foam rubber. He chilled immediately. His face was painful almost as soon as he bailed out. The sea had a slight glint of light from a quarter-moon. It was a clear night and beautiful stars shown above. From twenty thousand feet, at his rate of descent, it would take two minutes to reach the surface. He was rusty at jumping, so he checked his wrist altimeter often. At six thousand feet above sea level, he began holding his arms out and spreading his legs to slow his descent. When he could, he assumed a horizontal position in the air and that slowed him even more. He had tethered himself to a rucksack with the inflatable boat in it and other gear. It was bulky and descended at the same rate as he did. When he got ready to open his chute, he pulled the release on the tether and pulled the rip cord for the rucksack. Then he pulled his own chute's rip cord. The canopy popped open with a snap and suddenly he was decelerated to a much slower descent. He used the shrouds to circle so he could look for the November Victory. On the second turn, he spotted red and white lights below, meaning that he was looking at the port side of the bow of a ship. He hoped it was the November Victory and steered toward a position well in front of it. When he maneuvered into the path of the freighter, it was only about a half mile away and looked very big in the night. He could see two other men descending and watched them hit the water ahead of him and farther from the freighter than where he thought he would land.

Things happened fast. He made one last maneuver to position himself and saw the rucksack splash into the sea. He hit the surface with a smack about fifty yards from it and immediately shed his parachute harness and swam over to it as quickly as he could. Because of the cushioning of the water as he arrived, he was not injured, but it would have been an eventful arrival if he had landed on solid ground. The water was warm to the touch and the areas of his skin that had been chilled soon recovered normal warmth. The swim tired him and he was breathing hard when he got to the floating rucksack. He pulled the lacings open and pulled the inflatable out and immediately pulled the cord to inflate it. It bucked and shifted as it inflated and folded open on its middle. In about ten seconds, it was fully inflated and he rolled into it and pulled the rucksack into the raft with him.

He felt in the rucksack for the boarding hook and found it. He opened the sack and began assembling sections of the hook. With all the sections, it was over sixteen feet long, aluminum, but painted black. The shafts had sticky rubber coverings so he could climb up it better when it was wet. As he got it together, he looked again and found that the freighter was bearing down on him only about two hundred yards away. He slung his weapons pouch on his shoulder with his assault kit and secured it with its snaps and paddled quickly. It was clear that he would be approaching the freighter on its starboard side, so he got ready to use the boarding hook as he got close. The size of the freighter was impressive and he could feel the vibration from its propellers and its parting of the sea as it plowed toward him. At the proper time, he stood shakily in the inflatable and tried to snag the gunwale as it passed overhead. He was lucky and snagged the gunwale of the deck rim with his first attempt. As he was pulling himself up, a second hook snagged the gunwale about thirty five feet behind him. He kept climbing and soon was able to get a hand over the edge of the gunwale and pull himself up. He laid the boarding hook on the deck next to the rim and looked back to see if he could help the other man get aboard. He needn't have worried, because the other man was already swinging over the gunwale. They quickly crawled over to position between the hatches for the holds on the tops of the holds.

Chapter 51

Chuck Marsden was the last one out as they parachuted into the darkness. The night was clear enough that he could see the entire team spread out below him. He waited to pull the rip cord on the rucksack he had attached to him on a fifty foot elastic tether. Once the canopy opened, the descent rate would decrease a lot. He could stabilize once more and watch as the team descended toward the water. The surface conditions were ideal for their purposes, calm seas with just barely any swell. As they got to about ten thousand feet above the water, he could make out the November Victory plowing along in the night. He could see that several team members were enough ahead of the ship that they would probably be able to steer into its path and have a shot at boarding. They would need to hustle, though, to get their rafts inflated and their equipment in order in time to paddle over to the path of the oncoming freighter. What really concerned him was that it looked like he would drop into the water behind the freighter. He tugged on the shrouds to accelerate his speed even though it would cost him on his rate of descent.

Try as he might, it soon became obvious that he was not going to make it to a position from which he could try to board the November Victory. Now his main concern became avoiding notice by the submarine a mile behind. In a minute, he was just above the water and looked around just before he hit. He had seen nothing just before he hit. When he came to the surface, he quickly gathered the parachute and discarded it. It sank slowly after he cast it off. The equipment rucksack was floating nearby, so he swam over to it. He immediately opened the lacings and got out the one man raft. It was black and made no additional light in the night. He quickly inflated it and climbed aboard. He hauled the rucksack onto the raft and got out the paddle. He hooked the rucksack to the center thwart of the raft. A quick look at his wrist compass told him which way to face to look for the oncoming submarine. He heard it before he saw it. It was running at periscope depth and he could see the disturbance in the surface when it got within about a hundred yards. He bent over so as to display as little height at possible and waited. As the snorkel and periscope passed within forty feet of him, he held his breath. It went by without any deviation and the periscope did not turn to look back. He watched it out of sight. By now the November Victory was more than a mile ahead and he had no hope of overtaking it. Besides, any attempt might be picked up by the submarine. So he just relaxed and lay back in the raft, knowing that, on this mission, his participation was probably at an end. It would be four hours and a little before dawn, so he just watched the horizon for a while until he became drowsy and then took a nap.

Chapter 52

Meanwhile, Flynn, who had landed just two hundred yards in front of the ship, could not get into its path close enough to snag the gunwale with his hooked pole, missed getting on board and watched the ship go by from a frustrating fifty feet.

O'Hanson, the next farther one in front of the ship, was able to get alongside with his hooked pole and snagged the gunwale about half way back on the ship where the gunwales were closest to the surface of the ocean. He hung there while he got his rucksack secured to his ankle with its tether, then he pulled himself up to the gunwale with the pole. He peeked over the edge and saw no one on deck. He could see the lighted bridge, but no one appeared in the window, so he eased over the edge and got in front of the hatch that covered the rear hold. After he waited a bit to rest, he pulled the rucksack up by its tether and went over to the gunwale to heave it over onto the deck. He laid the boarding hook next to the gunwale and grabbed hold of the rucksack. Then he quickly pulled it over to his hiding position and waited to see if anyone else made it on board.

Lero just happened to be looking at the starboard side gunwale as another hook came over the edge. In a moment, O'Hanson came up and looked over the gunwale. He saw Fazio and Lero crouched in front of the hatch and pulled himself over onto the deck. He scrambled over to where they were hiding and waited to check to see if anyone had observed him boarding. When it looked clear, he pulled up his tethered rucksack and went quickly over to it and pulled it into the hiding place.

He scanned the deck and then quickly slipped over onto the deck. Fazio and O'Hanson watched as Lero pulled up his rucksack and dragged it over to join them in front of the hatch.

They waited fifteen minutes to see if any more of the team would make it on board. When no one did, they got out their weapons and equipment. It appeared as if they would have to access the hold from inside the ship, since the hatch was way too heavy for even the three of them to lift. Clearly, it would take a crane to lift the hatch cover on the hold, so they decided to access the hold from below. One man kept his assault rifle at the ready and led the group toward the hatch in the bulkhead in the front of the superstructure. The others had their rifles slung in front of them and snugged with an elastic strap to keep them from bumping into objects that would resound. The team edged up to the hatch. (NOTE: Dogs are handles that operate to snug a door on a ship to make it water tight. The surround the door and help to secure it.) The dogs around the hatch were all in the open position, except the one on the right side of the door.

O'Hanson turned the handle and peeked in when he had opened the door an inch. The dimly lit corridor was empty. He opened the door and stepped in. The rumbling ambient noise created by the ships motors and gear made it a challenge to communicate by whispers, but they knew that the ship's noise would drown out their voices if they kept them low. The old freighter hummed and moaned with the noise and vibration of its big diesel engines.

To the right of the door opening, was another opening that showed a ship's ladder extending below decks. They quickly and quietly went over and looked down. One flight down, about sixteen feet below, was another deck, also dimly lit. They descended the ladder quietly. In spite of the ventilators that took in air as the ship traveled and dumped it out at the stern, the passageway smelled of diesel fuel, sweat, cigarettes and kitchen odors. When O'Hanson got all the way down, he could see that the corridor assumed an "L" shape with a passageway across the ship to the far side and a corridor along the side of the ship forward and aft.

As they eased forward, they came to the hatch that would lead them into the aft hold. The dogs on the door were all in the locked position, and there was a large brass padlock on the door.

Fazio tapped Lero on the arm, indicating that he wanted to move ahead of Lero and look at the lock. He put down his rucksack and fished into it. He came out with a small khaki canvas bag about eight inches by twelve. He opened it and took out a small pencil flashlight and put on his short range glasses. After he looked at the lock for a few seconds, he selected two tools from the sack and went to work on the lock. He held the lock up off of the door with his knee and put his pencil flashlight in his mouth to shine onto the lock. He worked with both hands with the lock picks. In about twenty seconds, the lock came open. He quietly removed it from the door and put it in his bag, still open. He looked over at O'Hanson and Lero and nodded. They quietly opened the dogs on the hatch and opened the door. It was pitch black inside, so they quickly ducked inside and closed the door. Each man lit his flashlight and they began to look around. The hold was about fifty feet long and forty feet wide and sixteen feet high. It was crowded with crates and boxes and equipment, but on the side toward the bow, were the three crates they had come for.

O'Hanson signaled that he wanted to speak, so they all drew close.

"Do you think we should send one of us up to entrain the anesthetic gas into the air intakes?"

Lero and Fazio thought about it for a moment.

Lero said, "We have made it this far without disturbing anyone. There is so much ambient noise and vibration that I think we can go ahead and do our work on the triggers. We are not going to make any noise and it is very unlikely that anyone will disturb us in the middle of the night. But, I think one of us should stay by the door with a weapon at the ready while we work. It should not take too long."

Fazio and O'Hanson nodded. O'Hanson asked Fazio to guard the door for them and he nodded. They waited until he got into position and nodded, before they turned their attention to the crates.

O'Hanson took out a crowbar from his rucksack and carefully and quietly took the side off of one of the crates. Lero helped him lift the cover away and put it down silently on the deck. Lero took out his kit of tools and parts and began unscrewing the screws on the hatch that they located like Ernie told them to. Inside, the red, blue, yellow and white wires on the trigger ran from an attach point with securing screws back to the weapon's attach point. Lero took each wire loose and replaced it with the dead wires they had brought, red for red, and so on.

Next, he opened the interior hatch on the trigger and pulled out the circuit board second from the front. He put it in his sack and got out its neutering replacement. It slid into place with a bump that told Lero that it was fully inserted. He looked at his watch. It had taken twelve minutes to do the first one. They buttoned up the hatch with its screws and put the side back on the crate. It showed no signs of meddling. Fortunately, loading such a crate on a ship causes all sorts of small dings and gouges in a crate like this and this one was no different.

O'Hanson used his crowbar and opened the side of the second crate. They had to scoot it over a bit to get clearance enough to get the side panel out of the way enough to operate on the contents, though.

As Lero and O'Hanson were completing the alteration of the third trigger, Fazio saw the light change in the companionway outside the door, which he had left about two inches ajar. He could see a crew member approach. The man was carrying a large plastic garbage can of trash. When he saw the door ajar, he pushed it in and stepped in. He was astonished to see Fazio, in a black wet suit with an assault rifle pointed at him. Fazio put his finger to his lips to signal the man to remain silent. The man, so startled and shocked, just nodded and backed up. Fazio shut the hatch. Lero and O'Hanson looked up to see what was happening. They rushed to Fazio and the three men stood to one side and the crewman stood, shaking, a few feet away, obviously afraid for his life.

"What shall we do?" asked Fazio.

"Cover his mouth with duct tape and tie him up with tie wraps while we think this out," said Lero.

Once that was done and the three could get their heads together, they discussed the situation.

"Clearly, one option is to quietly throw him over the side. Cut his tie wraps and throw a one man raft after him, so he won't drown," said "O'Hanson. "But if we do, someone will find him and he will tell them what happened and the cat will be out of the bag. Disneyland will know that the weapons are suspect and will check them over thoroughly."

"Another alternative, is the leave him here, close the hatch, open the sea cocks, disable the valves, disable the pumps, so they cannot either shut off the sea cocks or pump out the water as it comes in, go overboard and let the ship slowly sink," said Fazio.

(Note: Sea cocks are valves that let ocean water into the ship for balance and to keep the ship in trim. Many times, the control wheels for the valves are on the deck or in the superstructure many feet above the valves and are connected to the wheels by rods or hollow pipes.)

Lero frowned as he considered the alternatives proposed and thought of others. Then he said, "Let's do a combination of both. If we leave him in a raft, he will be able to tell his superiors that the ship was sunk by commandos. I certainly don't want that information out there. On the other hand, we cannot just kill this innocent man in cold blood. Let's open the sea cocks, disable the pumps and spike the valves so they cannot close the sea cocks, keep his arms bound and mouth duct taped. Let's find out, if we can, what language he understands and tell him that if he cooperates with us, we will spare his life. We will take him with us, over the side and avoid the submarine tailing us by paddling away perpendicular to the heading of the freighter and the sub. At the speed we and sub are making, it will take the sub about five minutes to reach the position where we go over the side. We will need to paddle hard to get out of its sight. Once they are gone, somewhere out there, probably many miles from here, this ship will sink. If the sub spots it, they may pick up any survivors, none of which will be able to tell them anything about how the ship sank. The missing crewman will be assumed drowned with the ship."

Lero asked the men what they thought of his plan. O'Hanson and Fazio agreed that it was a good one under the circumstances.

Lero volunteered to stay with the prisoner while Fazio and O'Hanson opened the sea cocks, disabled the pumps and spiked the valve wheels where the sea cocks were controlled. After O'Hanson and Fazio slipped out into the companionway, Lero turned to the terrified man.

"Speak English?" The man shook his head "No."

"Parlez vous Francais?" Another "No."

"Hablan Espanol?" Yet another "No."

"Russkaya?" No response.

The man was clearly oriental. Lero asked in Tagalog, the Philippine language if he understood. The man did not respond. Then Lero asked in Mandarin (Chinese) if he spoke that language. The man nodded.

Lero told him that his life would be spared if he cooperated. The question on Lero's face was answered with a vigorous nod by the sailor.

Lero told him to remain quiet while they waited for the two men to return.

In about five minutes, Lero could hear water running and the deck of the hold was soon covered. The sea cocks were opened for this hold by one of his teammates. He waited as the water continued to rise. He could see that the lip of the hatch to the companionway was about six or seven inches above the deck, and it looked like it would only be a few minutes before the water would overflow the threshold. Fifteen minutes passed. Then O'Hanson came back in the hatch. Fazio was about a minute behind him. By now the water was five inches deep and rising. Objects were beginning to float in the rising water. Fazio and O'Hanson reported that the valve wheels had been removed and the control rods bent to they could not be easily repaired. They had found that there were pumps on each side of the ship, and they had removed the spark plugs, wiring and distributor caps from the motors. Even if the ship carried spares, which was very unlikely, it would take a while to repair the pump motors.

They gathered up their rucksacks, which each contained an inflatable raft and paddles and went out. Fazio replaced the lock and locked it. They sneaked back to the ladder and went up, taking the seaman with them.

When they got to the hatch leading to the deck, they checked to see if anyone were about. They could see men in the bridge, but the deck was dark and unlit.

They edged over to the gap between the hatches covering the holds and hid. Each man made sure he had his inflatable raft ready to inflate. They went over the side one at a time. The seaman was apprehensive about jumping into the ocean with nothing to ride in or hang onto. Lero pointed to the raft in his rucksack and with a sign told the man that he would be safe, so when it came his turn, the seaman obediently jumped into the passing foam of the ship.

They were immediately impressed with the boat's motion past them. Twelve knots might not seem like a lot compared to other boats, but when a three hundred foot long freighter is going past you in the middle of the night, the speed is pretty impressive.

Chapter 53

Lero and the seaman paddled away from the boat's side as they watched it pass. When it had passed them and they had ridden out the wake of the propellers, Lero pulled the inflatable raft out of the bag and inflated it. He and the seaman got in and immediately began paddling perpendicular to the path of the freighter. In five minutes, they managed to paddle a hundred yards or so. Since the sea was so calm, in the ambient light from the stars, they could see the periscope of the Russian submarine pass by. They paddled some more for twenty minutes or so, then stopped to rest and locate Fazio and O'Hanson.

Using his infrared filter on his flashlight, Lero swept the horizon with a steady light, then turned off the flashlight. He and the seaman looked about to see if there were any response. He saw a flash and returned its signal with a series of flashes.

They paddled in the direction they thought the light had come from for ten minutes, then paused and send out another sweeping signal of dashes. This time, the response came quickly and they paddled some more in the direction of the flashes. In a few minutes, they could see two rafts coming toward them.

Lero gathered the group together. He said, "Let's wait a good while here before we signal anybody. I want to give that Russian sub time to get well away from our position."

The men nodded their agreement.

Chapter 54

Boswell and Riley, who had parachuted with Lero and O'Hanson and Fazio, had been in front of the freighter when they hit the water, but they could not swim into the path of the freighter in time to grapple on and board. They had drifted behind in the freighter's wake. They found each other right away and were alternately watching the freighter depart and watching for the signs of the submarine's passage.

They saw the periscope coming through the water at them. There was a strange vibration in the water, too, from the propellers of the submarine.

Boswell said, "I have an idea, Follow me."

Riley nodded and they rolled out of their rafts and swam as fast as they could toward the periscope. It was sticking about three feet out of the water and they grabbed onto it below the lenses so they would not be seen. Water swept over them and almost overpowered them, but they clung tight. They wrapped a belt around the periscope and rode along. From time to time, they could see the freighter.

Boswell, pulled himself near to Riley and said, "Let's shinny down the periscope and plant our Semtex charges around the hatch on the conning tower. If we set the timer for an hour, we can be well away from it when it blows. If we are lucky and they don't have the watertight doors closed, we might just flood the ship before they know they have been hit."

"Sounds like an act of war, to me," said Riley. "Then he smiled and reached for his Semtex charges. Altogether, they had eight pounds. They rigged it all in a bundle with two detonators, both set for an hour, just in case one did not work. It all fit into a musette bag and made a nice satchel charge. The strap had a clasp on it where it could be opened and refastened. Riley and Boswell thought it would secure the bag around a ladder rung or a piece of the hatch hardware. Since they could feel the ladder rungs welded to the conning tower with their feet, they decide that one of them would go down, using the rungs to pull himself to the deck of the conning tower below them. Then, if he could see well enough with his underwater flashlight, he would fasten the satchel charge to the hatch and come back up.

"If this fails, they will turn around and search for us. We will be toast if they find us, not to mention that if we escape them, and are rescued, we will probably be court martialed and maybe jailed for a long time."

"Yeah, but how many swabbies can say that they sank a submarine single handedly?" asked Riley. "After all they are up to no good and they did ram us, didn't they?" He winked.

Boswell grinned and handed Riley the satchel charge. Riley checked the timer on each detonator and then flipped on his mask, took a deep breath to charge his snorkel with air and pulled himself under with his hands on the rungs of the ladder.

He seemed to be gone for quite a while, but just as Boswell began to be anxious about him, he quietly surfaced.

"We are good to go, Bos. Let's get off this tub before something happens.

Boswell smiled, nodded and they let go their strap around the periscope and trailed off in the slipstream. Both of them watched as the propellers slipped past them on the lower side of the stern. They could only see the foam created by the propellers and not the propellers themselves, but they were glad to be in the wake. They watched and swam for a few minutes.

Chapter 55

"Captain, come quickly," said the first officer. Captain Isamov threw off the blanket and jumped to his feet. During times of tension, he slept in his uniform. He ran with the first officer from his quarters to the conning tower. When he got there, the crewman manning the periscope saw him arrive in the conning tower and quickly moved aside so Isamov could look. What Isamov saw was astonishing. The November Victory was very low in the water, seawater was gushing over the gunwales. As he watched, the ship pitched forward and in a few seconds slipped beneath the water. Great sprays of water erupted as the ship went down. Isamov's eyes were wide open in astonishment.

"How could this happen?" he roared. "Did no one notice that she was low in the water?"

"No sir," said Vasily, the first officer. "It was dark and we did not detect the ship lowering in the water until it was quite far along."

"This is bad, Vasily, very bad. Sound general quarters, assemble a boarding party . Prepare to surface. We will look for survivors first, then try to get to the bottom of things. Note our position and the time."

"Yes, Captain," said the first officer and nodded to the chief boatswain's mate so he could sound general quarters. In a few seconds, the submarine went from a placid night shift to emergency status. Men scrambled into uniforms and boots.

Isamov went to his cabin and quickly composed a message to be transmitted with encryption:

"1911 hrs, UTC (Universal Coordinated Time, same as Greenwich meridian time), 20 September 2015, Urgent. Urgent. Regret to inform you that the November Victory sunk under mysterious circumstances approximately twenty minutes ago. A watch had been maintained by periscope from a distance of twelve hundred meters. No unusual activity was observed until the boatswain's mate reported the ship low in the water. When the Captain reached the conning tower, the November Victory pitched over and sank. The bC-43 will surface and conduct a search for survivors and any clue as to how the ship came to sink without warning. Position of the NV at sinking was 08.30.10 N , 109.08.00 E. Advise what action you wish us to take. Isamov."

He handed the message to the radioman and waited for what he thought would be a dreadful reply.

In a few minutes, the radioman received a signal and he printed it and handed it to the Captain.

"Remain the area until daylight. Continue search until satisfied no survivors. Return to V on surface, best speed. Await orders."

Isamov ordered that the sub circle and look for survivors at periscope depth, full alert with radar and sonar for approaching ships. Double watch in the conning tower. He ordered Commander Vasily to report any more bodies or anything else interesting and he retired to his cabin to wait out the night. He lay on his bunk with his mind in turmoil. He wondered if he would spend his retirement in the gulag.

Chapter 56

Boswell and Riley had been treading water for about an hour when they saw a flash of white on the horizon that quickly turned to red and then darkness again. The night returned to silence.

On the bC-43, there was a tremendous explosion. Water began flooding the conning tower immediately. Men were so startled that they froze in position. The water overwhelmed the men in the conning tower and the first officer was unable to give the order to close the watertight doors. Water continued to flood into the submarine. With no orders, everything continued as previously ordered. Everyone on the boat heard and felt the explosion. Isamov catapulted from his bunk, but by time he got to the companionway, the water was waist deep and rushing in. In a cascade of catastrophes, most of the water tight doors remained open and the boat flooded quickly. The aft torpedo room occupants had the presence of mind to close their water tight door, though.

Because the sub was submerged, the additional water prevented it from surfacing. No one had blown the ballast tanks to surface the ship, anyway. Now, no one could blow the ballast tanks because the sub was flooded so quickly. Everyone not holding onto something was swept to the rear. Those that were holding onto something were drowned quickly. Just before the boat completely flooded, the aft sleeping compartment hatch was closed against a strong stream of water by the men trapped there. Now twenty six men in the aft sleeping compartment and the aft torpedo room waited to find out what happened and how they would be rescued. In a few minutes, the sub nosed down and came to a halt because the propellers were out of the water. The bC-43 came to a stop with just the stern of the boat above water. Because the motors could not breathe air, they shut down. Then it got very quiet.

Chapter 57

Lero, Fazio , O'Hanson and the Chinese seaman saw the flash on the horizon. It was so far away that they did not hear a sound for a full minute.

"What do you suppose?" asked Fazio.

O'Hanson said "Could have been a distress flare, but the report took almost a minute to get here. That means it happened almost fifteen miles away. Must have been a pretty good sized blast if it was explosives."

Lero said, "Let's see if we can raise any other team members. Use your infrared filters."

They took out their flashlights and began flashing dashes into the night. After a few minutes, they spotted return flashes to the east. They paddled toward the flashes for a while, then signaled again. In about an hour, they met up with Riley and Boswell. Since they only had three rafts, and Boswell and Riley were without rafts, O'Hanson and Fazio took the men into their rafts. Now there were two men in each of the three rafts. The time was four forty five AM. Lero felt it was time to signal for rescue. Lero took out a satellite telephone and dialed. It hummed, buzzed and then rang. A voice answered with just "Hello."

"This is Lero. We need pickup. We are five plus a prisoner. Chinese. Will leave the line open until you have a GPS fix on us."

"Very well," said the voice.

After about three minutes, the voice said, "Your position determined. Exfiltration will be in approximately three hours."

Lero said, "Understood. Thanks."

The line went silent.

Since they thought the Chinese sailor could not understand what they were saying, they discussed what had happened. Boswell and Riley told Lero what they had done. There was a long silence.

After a pause, Lero said, "Fellows, we won't know the effect of what you did for a while. I think the rest of us should agree that we never heard you tell us what you just told us. This could have international repercussions. The quieter the better."

The men expressed their agreement.

The men did not know, of course, what type of exfiltration would take place, so they watched on the surface and in the air. Shortly after dawn, Fazio spoke up. "I see a ship to the north, sir." He pointed it out to the rest. Lero asked one of them to light a smoke grenade. In a minute, the wind began to disperse the purple smoke. It took about thirty five minutes for the ship to reach their vicinity. It was a Guided Missile Frigate, and when it got close, it hoved to and stopped in the water. A small inflatable was lowered and came to them quickly.

"Hello, there," sang out the boatswain as the raft neared the floating men.

"Our area commander said to pick you fellows up, if we could. We are from The Royal Australian Navy. Our ship's name is the Canberra. Come aboard."

Lero spoke for the group. "Thanks for the rescue. We are glad to see you fellows."

"How long have you fellows been in the water?" asked the boatswain.

"About eight hours," said Lero. "This fellow here is our prisoner. We will explain everything to your captain."

"Right o," said the boatswain and the mate turned the inflatable around and towed them back to the ship.

When they were safely aboard, the Captain came down to greet them.

"Welcome aboard the Canberra," he said. "I am Commander Honeywell. Sorry you lost your ship. Your man Jefe explained your plight to our area commander and he determined that we were the ship closest to your position. Glad we could give you a ride. We are going to Singapore and you can secure transport from there, I am sure. You must be thirsty and hungry. Do any of you require medical attention? My men will show you to the mess hall and will take your prisoner to the brig."

"Commander, I think a warm meal will bring all of us back to life. We are very grateful," said Lero, but, we have two men out there probably west of this location, on rafts. They came with us. Could you wait in this location and search a bit for them? They have flares and smoke grenades and are very competent seamen."

"Sure thing, Lero, you guys go below and get fed and warmed up and we will loiter here and go look for them."

"Thanks, Captain. I will grab some chow and rejoin you here if that is alright."

"Get some food and some stout coffee and come back," said the Captain.

Lero thanked him again and they fell in line behind the boatswain to go to the mess hall.

Chapter 58

(The following dialogue is in Maylay. The ship is the Maylasian Navy destroyer Arkabrat.)

'Captain, radar reports a ship still in the water, about eight nautical miles ahead and on a heading of two eight zero," the radioman relayed.

"Very well. Let's investigate. Come left to two eight zero and slow to one third."

"Aye, aye, sir," said the officer of the deck and relayed the orders.

In about ten minutes, the lookout spotted the submarine. "Submarine, off the port quarter, half a mile," he said.

The Captain trained his binoculars in the direction indicated and soon picked out the submarine.

"Looks like they have had trouble," said the captain to the officer of the deck.

"Yes, sir. I will send a raft over."

In a few moments, a raft was lowered and four sailors boarded to go over to the sub. By now, the destroyer was only about a hundred yards away and still in the water.

"Radioman, send this message to fleet command: 'Sighted partially submerged submarine at latitude eight degrees, thirty minutes, eight seconds, longitude one hundred nine degrees, ten minutes, ten seconds east. Checking for signs of life. Markings not visible at this time. Appears to be diesel electric and designed in the sixties. Will advise.'"

"Yes, sir. Right away," said the radioman.

The boatswain leaned over to the hull of the submarine and gave three taps with a brass hammer. In a few seconds, there were several vigorous taps from within.

The boatswain took out his transceiver and spoke into it, "Captain, we hear tapping from inside. There are survivors."

"Very well, said the captain. "Return to the ship pick up the mechanic and his equipment."

The inflatable raft quickly went back to the ship. A seaman was standing by with a small pallet of equipment. The men quickly loaded it into the raft, one seaman was left on the ship, so the mechanic would not overload the boat and they returned to the submarine.

As soon as the mechanic got to the hull, he took out a battery powered drill and a bit and drilled a hole into the hull of the submarine. Since the metal of the hull was about three quarters of an inch thick in that area of the hull, it took a while to drill. The mechanic had to put water on the drill bit twice to cool it before it went through. When it pierced the hull, air flowed out, so he immediately inserted a tap and using a tap wrench, threaded the hole he had just drilled. Then he inserted a temporary plug in that hole and drilled another hole about a foot from the original. He threaded the second hole, too and as soon as he did so, he started an air compressor and attached the hose to the nozzle in the first hole. Then he screwed a valve into the second hole and left it closed.

Now, the survivors would have a supply of fresh air.

He tapped out, in Morse code, "How many?"

In a few moments, came the tapped reply, "Twenty six."

The mechanic called on his radio to the Captain, "Sir, we have twenty six survivors. I have attached an air line, so they can breathe fresh air. What do you want me to do now?"

"Tell them we will rig a tow and tow them to shallow water. Too dangerous to attempt a rescue under these circumstances. Tell them it will be at least four hours."

"Aye, aye, sir," he said and tapped out a message to the trapped crew.

By now, a second raft had arrived pulling a pair of two inch hawsers. The seamen went over to the exposed propeller shafts of the submarine and attached the hawsers.

Both rafts returned to the ship and in a few minutes, the ship gently took up the slack in the hawsers and began to tow the submarine northerly at about ten knots. The Captain posted a watchman on the stern to keep an eye on the submarine to sound an alarm if it appeared to be sinking or if the hawsers broke.

The radioman spoke, "Captain, Fleet Headquarters advises that there is a small unnamed island forty three nautical miles north of our position."

"Very well," said the captain. Set course for north for now, all ahead one third and post a lookout to look for the island."

"Aye, aye, Captain," said the officer of the deck.

Chapter 59

Admiral Yoshenko, aide to the chief of Naval Operations, rushed into the office of Admiral Sergei Margolin, his eyes wide with apprehension and alarm.

"Admiral, our surveillance satellite picked up a transmission from the Commandant of the Malaysian Navy concerning a disabled and partially sunk submarine in the South China Sea. The captain of a Malaysian ship has radioed that he has the submarine in tow and is headed for an unnamed island to beach the sub where its surviving crew members can be extricated. Our intelligence apparatus, after I inquired, related to me that a Foxtrot class submarine from Vladivostok, operating on secret orders, was tailing a freighter with a secret cargo. The submarine in tow is probably the bC-43 that left Vladivostok with a crew of eighty six."

"Very disturbing, Yuri. Where is the freighter now? Where is our nearest submarine or surface vessel to the island in question?"

"I have inquired, sir, and I await an answer from Fleet Operations."

"When you find out, let me know immediately, Yuri."

"Yes sir," said Yoshenko and turned to follow up on the Admiral's orders.

Admiral Margolin turned in his seat to the globe he kept by his desk in the Kremlin. He rolled it over and into the sunlight streaming in the elevated window in the high wood paneled wall of his office. He took out a magnifying glass and examined the area where the sub was being towed.

In a few minutes, Admiral Yoshenko again appeared.

"Sir, we have a nuclear submarine, the Konovalof, two hundred nautical miles north north west of the subject island. What orders should I give?"

"Order the Konovalof to proceed at flank speed to the island, Yuri. Determine if the submarine under tow is ours and, if so, communicate to the captain of the ship towing the sub to allow our submarine to assist in the rescue of trapped sailors and the beaching of the submarine so a complete investigation may take place concerning the cause of the upset. Then find the nearest surface ship from our country or a friendly country to the freighter. Attempt to contact that ship and get them to look for the freighter. See if we have any other military ships in the area that we might divert to look for the freighter. See if we can get any information from our satellite people about the freighter's location."

"Immediately, sir," said Yoshenko and strode hurriedly from the room.

Chapter 60

On the Kanovalof, Captain Boris Malinkof turned to observe his radioman arrive hurriedly from the radio room.

"Sir, urgent message from Fleet Operations," and handed the captain the sheet with the message.

Malinkof glanced at the message for only a few seconds before he barked orders to his Exec.

"Alexi, go to flank speed, course of one six five degrees. Maintain our depth."

"Yes, sir," responded Commander Alexi Kochin and relayed the order to the sailors in charge of speed and course. The submarine responded almost immediately to the change in direction and speed. A throbbing hum that permeated the entire metal tube that was a Russian Alfa Class Nuclear Submarine rose in tone and volume.

"Assemble all officers in the ward room, Alexi, quickly."

Chapter 61

The Russian flagged tanker Okhosk Traveler was making its way easterly about one hundred nautical miles south east of Singapore, having just cleared the Malacca Straits. Its crew was relieved to be into the open sea and clear of the traffic that clogged the Straits.

The radioman came into the bridge in a hurry.

"Captain, we have received a most unusual message from our dispatcher," he said and handed the sheet to the Captain.

Captain Zabrisky took the sheet and walked over under a fluorescent light to read.

"What do you make of this, Mr. Myrdin?" asked the Captain.

"From what they say, the November Victory is about three hundred nautical miles ahead, roughly twenty degrees off our port bow on a heading of about zero eight zero. It is on a course of two five five at a speed of twelve knots. We should reach a point where will close with each other in about eight hours, assuming that they have provided us with its proper course and speed. They say that they will provide us with guidance information when we are close. I imagine that will come from a satellite or a high flying patrol plane. The instructions are that we are only to confirm that the November Victory is on course and is followed by a submarine. Such secrecy, Olaf. Must be something going on. Oh, well, we will set a proper course and advise me, please, if there are any further transmissions."

"Aye, aye, Captain," said Myrdin and ambled back to his radio room.

Zabrisky walked over to the seaman manning the wheel and instructed him to set a course of zero eight zero and hold speed at twelve knots.

The Okhosk Traveler lumbered on in the night.

Chapter 62

When Alita awakened, the first thing she saw was the lovely filigree plastered ceiling of their suite, but the first thing she smelled was the lemon in the tea cup that Harry was holding. He saw that she was awake and brought it over to her. He had opened the French doors of the suite and the sunlight was streaming in the parlor, but their bedroom was still shaded and dimly lit.

The telephone buzzed quietly. "Nice touch for a bedroom phone," thought Jefe as he answered.

"Yes," he said in a friendly way.

"Sir, this is the bell captain. A uniformed courier is here with a dispatch for you. May I send him up?"

"Yes, of course, Bell Captain. Thank you for your courtesy."

Jefe met the courier at the door a few minutes later. The young soldier stepped in and saluted and handed him a manila envelope.

Jefe thanked him, signed for the dispatch and said that he need not wait for a reply. The young man thanked Jefe and left.

Jefe carried the envelope into the bedroom and over to a table in the sitting area. As an added layer of security, he and Lero had worked out a list of code words and phrases so they could communicate discreetly. He sat in his robe at the table and opened the envelope. There was a string of several words, no address, no signature.

Jefe reached for his brief case and took out his code book. It was disguised as a paperback novel, but the words he wanted to see were on previously decided upon pages which he turned to. The first word in a line corresponded to the last word in the same line. Only he and Lero had similar books.

He got out a sheet of hotel stationery and put it on the glass top of the table. That way, what he wrote would not be imprinted on any subsequent sheets of a note pad.

He wrote the words of the message in one column and then began to look up the words they corresponded to in the novel. When he had finished, he could read the message.

"Three boarded modifications made discovered took one prisoner attempted sabotage ship escaped believe not observed picked up by friendlies two missing will search daylight check status of target blueberry."

The last word was a code word they had chosen to include in messages to indicate that no one had intercepted the code book, deciphered it and tried to send a diversionary or false message.

"Is everything okay?" asked Alita.

"Yes, so far so good," said Jefe.

"I will need to go to Wesley's office to check on things and relay a message or two," he said.

"Do you need to rush off?" she asked with a warm smile.

She was a picture, standing there in her beige pumps with her tea cup on one hand and the saucer in the other with the morning sun shining on her.

"First things first," he said as he reached for her. She moved over closer to him. Seated, he put his hand on the back of her neck and caressed her back all the way down, slowly. "Lordy she is shaped nicely," he thought, or maybe it was just that she fit his hands like she were made for them.

Chapter 63

Wesley was waiting when Jefe got to his office. The sign on the door said First Secretary.

"Good morning," he said.

"Good morning. Hope all is going well," said Wesley.

"Just fine, thanks. May I use your scrambled satellite phone?"

"Of course, use the one in my private office over there," as he pointed.

He dialed a long international number. After the usual buzzes, squeaks and whistles, it rang.

"Hello," was the only answer. No accent. No inflection in the woman's voice.

"This is Jefe. I need to talk to the observations officer assigned to support Unit Forty Seven."

Jefe had dialed the desk officer at the Overhead Observations department of the National Reconnaissance Office.

"What is your authorization, please?" she asked in a soothing voice.

"Turkey Hunt," he said.

"Hold a moment, please," she said and the line changed tone.

In a moment, the line was answered. "This is Major Hornady, can I help you?"

"This is Jefe. Just inquiring if you have any observations of the ship involved in Turkey Hunt, or its follower for me."

"It is just after dawn at the site, sir. We see no trace of the freighter where it should be, assuming consistent course and speed. Our analysts spotted a destroyer sized ship towing what appears to be a submarine northerly from the area."

"Have our elint or sigint fellows picked up any distress calls?"

"No sir, all seems quiet in that area."

(Note: Sig int is signals intelligence, usually intercepted telephone calls, faxes, texts, emails, etc. Elint in electronic intelligence, usually coded messages, radio transmissions, telemetry from satellites, intercepted messages sent by fiber optic cables, et.)

"Anything from search and rescue?"

"Search is under way by an Australian frigate for two sailors believed overboard from a ship in the same area as the freighter, sir. Nothing reported so far."

"Very well, Major Hornady, thanks very much. Have a good day."

"You, too, sir. Good day."

Jefe went back out into the outer area of Wesley's office.

"Everything work okay?" he asked.

"Sure, thanks for the use of your equipment. "

"Let me know when you need anything, Harry, and enjoy your visit to Singapore. Any adverse effects for your companion after the dust up on Thursday?"

"No, she has amazing powers of recuperation. What is the status of the robber?"

"Fellows at the hospital were not able to save him. Autopsied, finger printed and held for ten days. If no one calls for the body, we will bury him at sea."

"The streets are dangerous, aren't they? Same the world over," said Jefe.

"Yes, the drug culture makes for more desperation, I think," said Wesley. "No need to tell Alita about the chap, though."

"Thanks, Wesley. I will not mention it, but I am very grateful for the way you and your people handled the situation."

"Not at all, my friend," said Wesley.

Jefe shook his hand and said "I will stay in touch," and left.

Chapter 64

His military aide told the President that Admiral Bostock wanted to speak to him on the secure phone. When he answered, Bostock identified himself with his code word. President Thompson cautioned him to be careful what he said, so the conversation was rather cryptic. Basically, Bostock said he needed to talk to the President "quietly." President Thompson invited Bostock to come to the White House office so they could stroll in the garden. Bostock said he would come right away and the line went silent.

In twenty minutes, Bostock presented himself to the appointments secretary, Wilma Rudman. The President had told her to expect Bostock and to let him into the Oval Office right away.

She nodded to Bostock and said, "Go right in, Sir. He is expecting you." She simultaneously buzzed the President, who rose and started toward the door to greet Bostock.

"Thanks, for seeing me so quickly, Mr. President," said Bostock.

"What is it, Charles," the concerned President asked.

"I need to update you on the situation with Lero. Can we take a stroll?"

"Sure," said the President and motioned Bostock toward the door. After they went down the walkway and the stairs to the garden, they stood very close and Bostock said in very quiet tones, "Mr. President, our overhead reconnaissance people report that a Malaysian destroyer is towing the Russian submarine north toward an island. The sub is partially submerged and has been damaged. The radio reports from the ship say that their mechanics have determined that there are survivors on board and they are being supplied with fresh air as the sub is being towed. They plan to beach the sub at high tide and rescue the sailors. But there is another troubling development. A Russian tanker, the Okhosk Traveler has changed course and is heading toward the last known position of the November Victory. Also, we believe that a Russian nuclear sub has been dispatched to the area. Our guys have two men in the water who could not board the November Victory. They will be searching for them from the Royal Australian corvette Canberra. Lero and his two men took a sailor prisoner from the November Victory. All indications are that the November Victory sank at about zero five hundred yesterday morning with all hands, except the prisoner. Our concern now is that the Russians, either the tanker or the sub will find our men before we do. Our sub, the West Virginia,   is on its way at flank speed to the site, as well, but it is over three hundred nautical miles to the east at this time. This could shape up as an international incident. However, with the November Victory missing, none of its crew could report our boarding. It is believed by Lero and his crew that their activities on board were not observed."

"We have dispatched a spotter plane from the Reagan and it should be reaching the area any time now. It will have a loitering capacity of about an hour and a half, but we will send another plane to keep up the surveillance as that one has to leave."

"On another subject, sir, we are monitoring all the cell phone traffic picked up in the White House and our decryption guys are looking for the key words we inserted into dialogue."

"Thanks for coming so promptly, Charlie, and thanks for the update. Keep me informed and stay in the situation room today, will you? I want your eyes on this situation."

"Sure thing, Mr. President. I will update you as I get further information."

The two men walked back up the stairs and into the Oval Office. Bostock walked straight through and went downstairs to the Situation Room.

Chapter 65

Bernie Maroney and Marsden had been separated by about two miles when the November Victory passed. Maroney was too far laterally to get into a boarding position in time and watched the ship and the submarine pass by in the night. Marsden missed the ship and the sub because he landed in the water behind the ship and dodged the submarine to avoid detection. In the night, using their infrared strobes and goggles, they were able to spot each other and paddle toward each other. Now, after about two hours of paddling, they met up.

"How many do you think made it to the ship, Bernie," asked Marsden.

"I saw two that landed between me and the ship. I saw one was definitely going to land in the sea behind the ship before I hit the water," said Bernie.

"We may be here for a while. Why don't we turn on just one of our EPIRBs and save the other one for later," said Marsden.

"Good idea," said Bernie. "You go first and we will save mine for another try if we need it."

At first light, about zero six thirty, they heard a turboprop plane high overhead. Bernie turned on his aircraft handheld transceiver onto the international emergency frequency, one hundred twenty one point five kilohertz and broadcast: "Mayday, mayday, mayday. This is India Two Four. Two survivors in the water. Request rescue."

In few seconds, a voice replied, "India Two Four, this is Strawberry Seven. Will relay your location to air-sea rescue. Will drop spare inflatable and emergency rations by parachute."

Bernie keyed the mike button and said, "Thank you, Strawberry Seven. Can you drop a pizza?"

"Negative, India Two Four, just the usual emergency rations, some fresh water, a radar reflector, and the usual provisions. Expect rescue in approximately eight hours."

"Thanks, Strawberry Seven."

"Strawberry Seven will loiter above you for another hour, then we will be replaced by another aircraft. Will advise."

"Roger that, Strawberry Seven. India Two Four standing by."

Bernie and Marsden saw the red and white rescue colored parachute at the same time and began paddling toward where they thought it would splash down as it descended. By now, it was mid-morning and the tropical sun was making them very warm in their wet suits, so they shed them and donned coveralls.

They had to paddle about twenty minutes to reach the rescue package which floated dutifully in the swells. They opened the end of the package and got out the larger inflatable and inflated it. Now they had a more comfortable boat and it had a canopy to ward off the sun's rays. Marsden set up the radar reflector which, with its ten foot aluminum pole, would make them visible to any radar on a surface ship within twenty miles. Any aircraft could spot it from a hundred miles, though.

Maroney and Marsden were resting comfortably in their inflatable. It was big enough for several people and they did not suffer for room. The boat had an overhead canopy that was open on all sides, so they could look for their rescuers and still have shelter from the sun. As they watched, a large submarine surfaced about half a mile to their west. Through their binoculars, they soon recognized the lettering on the conning tower as Russian. The silhouette of the conning tower was so similar to the American designs that it would not have been readily recognized as Russian unless they had seen the lettering and the gold seal on the front of the conning tower.

"Strawberry Seven, this is India Two Four, we have a buttermilk submarine surfacing about a half mile to our west. Suggest you alert Volcano."

"Roger, India Two Four, stand by."

Lieutenant Barrone turned the communications radio to another frequency and broadcast, "Volcano, Volcano, this is Strawberry Seven. India Two Four reports that a submarine with buttermilk markings has surfaced half a mile west of their position. Its intentions unknown."

(NOTE: Buttermilk is the code designation for Russia.)

"Roger, Strawberry Seven. Stand by."

"Strawberry Seven, this is Volcano. Descend and orbit within sight of India Two Four. Keep us informed."

"Roger, Strawberry Seven."

The submarine started toward the raft at a crawl. When it got within about two hundred yards, the deck officer hailed the raft: "Ahoy, the raft. We will come alongside and take you aboard."

Maroney fashioned a megaphone with some thick plastic sheets from the package that was dropped to them.

"Ahoy, submarine. We have rescue enroute. We do not wish to be taken aboard your ship."

There was a tense silence of several minutes. Then, men began to come out of a hatch at deck level from the conning tower. They brought out a large rolled up object that they unrolled and inflated into a large raft. They put the raft over the side and climbed down a portable ladder to the raft and made ready to come over to the raft where Maroney and Marsden were.

"Ahoy, the raft. We do not wish to be boarded, keep your distance," said Maroney. He and Marsden had gotten out their weapons from their waterproof containers and had locked loaded magazines in each.

The Russians replied, "Lower your weapons. We intend to board you."

"Ahoy the raft. Come no closer or you may be fired upon. Stand off."

By now the Russian raft was a hundred fifty yards from Marone and Marsden. A sailor in the bow of their raft began firing tear gas grenades toward Maroney and

Marsden. The grenades landed in the water and began emitting misty smoke that wafted toward their raft.

Things grew more tense as the Russian raft drew closer. Now it was only fifty yards from Maroney and Marsden, who gripped their assault rifles and prepared to defend themselves.

There was a quickly rising whistling sound from the east. Everyone was surprised and jumped back in surprise when a Navy F/A 18 Hornet buzzed the Russian raft only about twenty feet above the water. The sonic boom that followed the fighter actually blew some of the Russian sailors out of their raft. Some of the others jumped into the water and began swimming quickly back toward the submarine. Maroney and Marsden used the distraction to paddle farther from the submarine as the fighter flew a tight circle, now at an altitude of about a thousand feet. It was clear that the fighter was checking for the effect of his first pass and preparing for another. As the sailors reached the submarine, the fighter made another pass between Maroney's raft and the submarine. The appearance of a fully armed F/A 18 at that speed, that close to the water was IMPRESSIVE.

"India Two Four, this is Ramparts, the aircraft. Are you guys OK? Any wounded?"

"Ramparts, this is India Two Four. We are fine. Thanks for cleaning out our earwax. That was very impressive. The Ruskies are going back to the sub. We will have to wait to see what they are going to do next. How long can you loiter?"

"The meter says I have twenty six minutes of loiter time until bingo fuel. A replacement will appear before I leave. Does the sub seem hostile now?"

"Negative, Ramparts. They are scrambling, but we need to wait to see what their next move will be. How soon can we expect surface rescue?"

"India Two Four, the Australian corvette Canberra with your other team mates on board is heading for your position, now twenty knots away. Expect them to arrive within an hour. Will inform them of the presence of the buttermilk sub. Do you have adequate weapons to repel boarders?"

"Thanks, Ramparts. Appreciate the information. We have assault rifles and some grenades. We sure do appreciate you today."

Marsden and Maroney scanned the horizon and spotted the small image on the horizon. With the curvature of the earth, they could only see about twelve miles on the surface, but the ship projected enough above the surface that they could make out part of its image on the horizon. It appeared to be coming directly at them.

By now the Russian sailors had taken the inflatable back to the sub, after picking up the sailors who had been knocked out of the raft by the pressure wave of the passing F/A 18 or who jumped out. The sailors left the raft on a tether and scrambled back up the ladder and went into the hatch on the conning tower. There was an ominous silence.

Obviously, the sub could pick up the contact of the arriving ship, so the sub just sat there. Probably its officers were communicating with their command structure for instructions.

Chapter 65

Captain Honeywell summoned Lero to the bridge. Lero went up at the double. The question on his face was answered by Captain Honeywell.

"We have sighted your men in an inflatable raft, but a Russian submarine has surfaced near them and is attempting to take the men on board. They have refused to be boarded or taken on board the sub and there is a stand-off. We may need to negotiate with the officers of the sub. They will have small arms, but this is a nuclear sub that is only armed with missiles. Our ship, though much more primitive, is equipped with five inch guns, twenty millimeter guns and fifty caliber machine guns, so we have superior tactical fire power. Please stay on the bridge with me while this unfolds."

"Will do, Captain," said Lero and picked up a pair of heavy binoculars.

In a few minutes, the corvette hoved to with the raft between it and the sub. The Captain gave orders for a crew to make an inflatable ready to go over to the raft where Maroney and Marsden were waiting.

The speaker on the Russian sub crackled and a voice broadcast: "Ahoy, this is Russian Submarine Kanovalof. We intend to take these men on board for questioning. A ship of Russian registry has disappeared and we believe these men may be involved in its disappearance."

There was a pause. Then Honeywell picked up his microphone and tripped the switch to power up the speaker system.

"Ahoy, Kanovalof, this is Royal Australian Navy Corvette Canberra. These are our men and we intend to recover them. Stand off."

"Mr. Showen, order the turret chief to train the main turret on the submarine and load his guns. Have the twenty millimeter crew and the fifty caliber crew to make ready."

"Aye, sir," said Showen and scurried to pass along the order.

Honeywell picked up his headset for the scrambled satellite link.

"Fortress West, this is Canberra. We have a situation. We are attempting to recover some survivors in an inflatable boat. A Russian submarine has surfaced across from us and is demanding to take these men on board for questioning in regard to the disappearance of a Russian flagged freighter last night. These men are part of Group 47 of the American military and we have the remaining four members of the unit on board.

Cannot determine the level of hostility we may encounter. Request permission to fire upon the sub if we are fired upon or hostile intent is shown. Over."

"Roger, Canberra, this is Fortress West. Stand by."

The Captain and Lero waited tense minutes as the commandos bobbed in their inflatable raft between the ship and the submarine. Several sailors came out onto the deck of the submarine with rifles and machine guns.

Below the bridge, on the foredeck, the main turret whined as it rotated sixty degrees to the starboard and lowered its guns to point at the submarine.

(Note: During World War II, ships armorers learned that it was sometimes necessary to lower guns below the horizontal, so provisions were made in later commissioned ships to allow the guns to be lowered this far.)

Both the twenty millimeter emplacement and the fifty caliber emplacement turned their guns to train them on the Russian sub. Roughly one hundred fifty yards separated the ships, with the inflatable with Maroney and Marsden on it bobbed almost half way between them.

The Russian submarine's speaker crackled again. A voice spoke in heavily accented English: "Canberra, do you have an officer who speaks Russian to meet with our representative?"

Lero, who was standing nearby, had deferred to Captain Honeywell, but now spoke up.

"Captain, may I make a suggestion?"

"Certainly, sir. What is your suggestion?"

"I speak Russian. Let me negotiate with the Russians. Would it be possible for me to borrow a uniform? I will go over and talk with them."

"This is obviously a tense situation, Lero. It is a real stretch of propriety to let you wear our uniform, and I may be court martialed for allowing you to do so, but under the circumstances, you are much more qualified to negotiate with the Russians than any of my crew."

Honeywell turned to his Exec. "Have an officer of similar size and build give Lero a uniform and cover, quickly."

"Aye, sir," said the Exec, Mr. Showen, and hurried to comply.

In a few moments, a Commander of the Australian Navy appeared. Since he was almost the same size and build as Lero. He saluted the Captain and he and Lero moved over to the corner of the bridge where he immediately began to remove his uniform and Lero began to remove his coveralls. The Commander helped Lero dress in the Royal Australian Navy uniform and a corpsman gave the Commander an Australian Navy coverall to put on. In a few minutes, Lero approached the Captain in his borrowed uniform.

"Do you have any advice or instructions for me, Captain?" he asked.

Captain Honeywell said, "This is a tense situation, Lero. I certainly hope you can get your men without any hostilities, but don't give them up. We are ready for action, if the situation presents itself. In the urgency of the moment, if you detect that they intend to fire on us, raise your left arm full length and dive overboard. Your raised arm will signal us that you detect that they intend to fire on us and that it is alright for us to fire on them. Please be careful and don't get hurt. Take an air-band transceiver with you if you want."

Lero said, "You may need my correct name sometime soon, sir, in case there are hostilities. My name is Dan Roman. Thank you for your trust. I will do my best."

"I know you will, Dan," said the Captain and shook hands with Lero.

Honeywell keyed the mike button on the speaker system and said, "Ahoy, Kanovalof. We are sending over an officer to meet with your representative."

Lero followed a sailor to the deck where a ladder had been lowered so Lero could board an inflatable raft with a seaman manning the outboard motor. There was a stand in the middle of the deck where Lero could hold on while he was being transported. The sailor motored away from the Canberra smoothly and took Lero first to the inflatable where Maroney and Marsden waited. The sailor drew up his inflatable next to the raft where Maroney and Marsden were.

"You guys okay?" he asked.

"Yes, sir," they each answered.

"This is a bit tense. The Russians obviously suspect that you had something to do with the disappearance of their ship. Since you were not able to see it, I can tell you that the November Victory mysteriously sank in the night last night. Our other crew members and a Chinese speaking prisoner are on board the Canberra. I am going over to talk with the Russians. If things get out of hand, better get in the water fast. The Canberra is ready to fire if necessary. Good luck, fellows. See you in a while."

Marsden and Maroney nodded soberly and watched Lero ride toward the sub.

When they reached the submarine, two sailors had been dispatched to moor and hold onto his inflatable while he boarded the submarine. They nervously saluted him as he got close and he returned their salute. They took hold of the grips built into the inflatable and Lero stepped onto the rope and wood ladder that extended upwards to the deck of the submarine.

He climbed carefully, holding onto the ropes at the sides of the ladder until he got so high on the sub that the curvature allowed him to stand upright and walk to the deck. A solitary Russian officer stood waiting for Lero.

As he approached, the Russian came to attention and saluted. Lero stopped a few feet in front of the Russian, came to attention and returned his salute.

(Note: All dialogue on board the submarine is in Russian.)

"Good day, sir. Welcome aboard the Russian Submarine Kanovalof. I am Major Yuri Voshenko."

"Good day, Major Voshenko. I am Commander Dan Roman. Thank you for your hospitality."

Voshenko stepped closer and shook hands with Lero.

"This is a most delicate situation, Commander. A Russian flagged freighter sank last night about forty miles west of here, under mysterious circumstances. We suspect that these men may know something about the sinking and we want to interrogate them."

Lero replied, "I am sorry about the loss of your ship, Major, but we heard a brief distress call last night. We could not tell what ship it came from and we deployed several inflatables with men to search for survivors. No survivors have been found and we were retrieving our searchers when your submarine appeared. We would be glad to assist you in the search for survivors if you would allow us."

"Thank you, Commander. May I ask you to wait a moment while I confer with my Captain?"

"Of course, Major. You and I have a duty to defuse this situation if possible. We mean no hostililty, but only want to protect our men."

They exchanged salutes and Major Voshenko turned and went into the hatch in the side of the conning tower. Captain Honeywell, his crew, and Lero's men watch tensely as the silence ensued.

"Pacific Command, this is Captain Malinkof of the Kanovalof. A Royal Australian Navy Commander from the corvette Canberra, has come aboard and conferred with our Major Voshenko. They maintain that the men in the raft between our two ships are members of the Australian Navy who were deployed in rafts last night to look for survivors after they received an abbreviated distress call. The distress call did not identify the sender, so it may have been the November Victory or our submarine bC-43. The Canberra has trained its guns on our submarine and we have no deck gun or other surface armament to counter the threat. Request instructions. Standing by."

There was a pause of three minutes.

Then the radio receiver came to life again.

The screen displayed the response of the Pacific Command: "Captain Makinkof of the Kanovalof. Clearly not a situation where we could prevail. Release the men in the raft and withdraw. Extend compliments to the Captain of the Canberra and the officer who came on board the Kanovalof. Continue search and report regularly."

Captain Malinkof asked Major Vashenko to come over and read the dispatch directly. Vashenko did so, and looked at Malinkof and nodded. He turned and went back onto the deck to confer with Lero.

"My orders are to release your men and extend our compliments to your Captain, Commander. Thank you for helping us defuse a difficult and tense situation."

Lero said, "Very well, Major. Thank you for your courtesy and hospitality. It has been a tense situation, indeed. We will retrieve our men and withdraw. I wish you a long and happy life."

They exchanged salutes and Lero climbed back down into the raft. The sailor returned the raft to the raft where Maroney and Marsden waited anxiously.

"Men, we are good to withdraw to the Canberra. Throw us a line and we will tow you," said Lero.

Maroney and Marsden smiled and nodded and did so.

In ten minutes, they were all on board the Canberra and the rafts were recovered. Because the angle between the ships permitted it, the Canberra dipped its flag momentarily as an international courtesy, and came to "all ahead one third." The two ships drew apart as the submarine got under way as well.

The Canberra had a cylindrical lead lined satellite communications antenna, so there would be no stray transmissions. Lero went to a quiet corner of the bridge and made the call. There were the usual buzzes, moans and creaks in the earpiece, but then it rang like a normal telephone.

"Hello," said the lady's voice.

"This is Lero. I need to speak to the Pacific Duty Officer, please."

"Hold a moment, please," she said.

"This is Major Shannon, Lero, how may I help you?"

"Sir, I need you to relay a message to Mr. Murfree for me, please."

"Right, go ahead, slowly with your message, so I can write it down."

"Tell Mr. Murfree that the groundhog saw his shadow, Chapter One of The Count of Monte Cristo, Mount Rushmore in the rain and Snow White is smiling. Tell him also that we are being well treated by the crew of the Royal Australian Navy corvette Canberra."

NOTE TO INSIDERS: This coded message meant that the ship had to be sunk, that they have one prisoner, that they believe that they were not detected and that all members of the mission crew are safe.

"Thank you, Lero. I have it. Your reply will probably come directly from Mr. Murfree. Good evening."

"Good evening to you, too, sir. Thanks." The line went silent.

Lero and his men went below to their bay to change clothes and de-brief. Lero stayed with his men as they each told what they had done and encountered. He recorded their statements so they could be incorporated into his report.

As all this was happening, Lero received a text on his satellite telephone, which read: "You know, sometimes the culmination of a mission is in a blinding flash of an explosion, and other times it is in the swirling gurgle of a quietly sinking ship. I am so glad you got this one done with no loss of life. Maybe it would be better to turn the guys loose in Singapore and give them some expense money. They can come back one at a time or by two's so as not to arouse any suspicion. Thank them and tell them we appreciate their willingness to risk it all for our country. The other matter we discussed needs an outside touch. Come straight in. Have Jean come in, too. Take care. Thanks."

Chapter 66

Next, he called Jean.

"I'm so glad to hear from you. I try not to worry, but I have been out there with you enough times that I know the dangers you face. Where are you? Can you tell me? When are you coming home?" she asked.

"I love you, Jean. I am fine. I can't tell you where I am, but I am in friendly hands. We are coming home. No one got hurt. We won the ball game. I will call you when we get to where I can do so without a security problem," he said.

"I'm so glad," she said. "I will be waiting. Be safe. I am so glad about the ball game. I love you."

"I love you, too," he said.

Later, after a good hot meal in the mess hall, Lero wandered into the lounge. There was a satellite-served television in the corner. He walked over near it. Most of the men were paying it no attention, just enjoying a little after dinner talk and exchanging the usual talk of sailors at sea.

The television was tuned to Al Jazeera. Lero watched and listened as the hijab clad lady read the news.

"Russian Navy public relations announced from Sevastopol this afternoon that a Russian submarine had been attacked in the Straits of Malacca, south of Singapore. They did not precisely name the alleged responsible party, but hinted that they think their sub may have been rammed on purpose by a western nation's submarine which had been tailing the Russian sub for some time. The Russians said that there were numerous casualties and some survivors. They are investigating with the help of the Malaysian Navy which helped tow the damaged sub to a dry dock."

Chapter 67

Jefe and Alita were enjoying a sumptuous dinner in the security and quiet of their suite, when the satellite phone rang.

"Hello," he answered.

"It's me. Say the word," said Lero.

"Sedona, is the good word. What is your good word?"

"Houston," said Lero.

"What's up?" asked Jefe.

"The stock market is going through a correction. The chicken coop is full. Nice day for a ride. I miss Tex Ritter. Dessert is plum pudding."

Jefe made notes for later deciphering.

"So glad to hear from you. You must come and see us sometime soon. Will comply with your request. Have a nice evening."

"You, too. Good evening."

Jefe pressed the "send" button on the satellite phone to turn it off. Then he rose and got out the novel with the code words in it. Laying in on the table cloth next to his notes, he decoded the message from Lero. Alita sat silently, but interestedly across from him. While she waited, she refilled his glass with Merlot.

"The words "stock market" meant "ship." Correction meant "sunk." "Chicken coop" meant his team. "Full" meant "no casualties." "Nice day" meant "in friendly hands." "Ride" meant "friendly ship." "Tex Ritter" meant "waiting for orders." "Plum pudding meant "mission accomplished."

"Is it good news?" asked Alita, unable to contain her curiosity any longer.

"Yes, it is good news. Nobody hurt and they got the job done. I will tell you more later."

"I am so glad. Does that mean that we will be going home soon?"

"Yes, after we take care of a few details. Maybe in a day or two."

They adjourned to the sitting area of the parlor. There was a television in the corner. They usually did not watch much television, but turned it on to lounge a while after a great dinner.

The channels available in Singapore included many from other countries. Just by chance, the set was tuned to the largest Malayasian station from Djakarta. The news included a few local items and then the announcer said in heavily accented English, "the Russian Official information agency reports that a Russian Submarine was substantially damaged in a collision with an unknown ship in the eastern Malacca Straits sometime in the night Wednesday. Malayasian Navy ship Arkabrat responded to the distress calls and is towing the partially submerged submarine to a nearby island to beach it for repairs. Further reports will be forthcoming."

Alita asked, "Does that have anything to do with our friends?"

Jefe nodded.

"You must catch me up with all this when you feel secure to do so," she said.

"I will be glad to," he said.

"That lovely dinner and the bottle of Merlot have made me somewhat sleepy. I think I will take a nice warm bath before I go to bed," she said. "I noticed that they supplied this suite with some very high quality bath salts."

She stood and asked, "Will you take care of my gown, while I draw a bath?"

"I would be honored," he said.

With that approval, she pulled her gown over her head and folded it double and carefully handed it to him. She then walked slowly to the bathroom clad only in her three inch tan pumps.

Jefe wondered what he had done to deserve such a beautiful woman in his life as he walked to the bedroom to disrobe and join her.

Later that night, as she slept soundly with her nose near the inner end of his left collarbone, Jefe reached a bit to the bedside table and retrieved his cell phone. The moonlight streaming in the window gave the room a slightly blue tint. He input a message to Barstow, the team leader: "Team meeting at 1000." He put the cell phone back on the bedside table and looked down at Alita as she gently breathed on his chest. "Thank you, Lord," he said as he lay back on the pillow.

Chapter 67

Consistent with their agreement that she would not leave the suite while he went to the team meeting, she had dressed in her favorite casual pants suit and took her tea cup with her to the sitting area to watch television while he was gone.

The taxicab maneuvered him through the chaotic Singapore traffic as quickly as it could. Once, the cab had to halt while a merchant with a load of fresh corn on a wagon pulled by a pair of water buffalo crossed the road on his way to market.

The building was in the business district of Singapore and was four stories high. He paid the taxicab driver and watched him drive off as he walked to the entrance. His key let him into a small interior hall, with a sturdy door just eight feet ahead. He knew from previous use that there was a closed circuit camera above the door to survey the hallway. He also knew that the insertion of his key in the lock would sound a subtle alarm for the occupants to be on the alert. Once they could see that it was Jefe, they put down their weapons. As instructed, all six team members were there. He motioned them to sit and took a straight backed chair at the table around which they sat.

"Things like this happen once in a while, fellows. Your teammates have succeeded in their efforts and we will not need to assault the ship from here. As far as you are concerned, we want you to stay a couple of days and go home in ones and twos, using different airlines."

Greg Callicoat, the team's oldest operator asked, "Jefe, what do you want us to do about the money?" Jefe could see the disappointment and concern on their faces.

"I will give you all enough money to buy tickets home and some walking around money for the next two days. As for the contract money, it is yours to keep, but we may make an adjustment in your compensation if we need your help in the future, so consider the money sort of a pre-payment."

"That is very generous of you, sir," said Callicoat and the rest nodded and said so, too.

"Just knowing you were ready to go for us was a great comfort. Have a safe trip home. As you understand, I cannot share much more information with you, but you have our sincere thanks. I can tell you that the other team had some difficulty, but achieved the goal and did not suffer any casualties. Lero, who is the chief of Unit Forty Seven wanted me to thank you personally." He rose and shook hands with each man.

As he rode back to the hotel in the taxicab, he felt the burden of the mission lift off of his shoulders. It was a great responsibility to send men into harm's way and he always felt great relief when a mission was over, especially when the men all came back with no injuries.

Chapter 68

The motor pool Suburban pulled up behind the white Grand Cherokee in the car port. Lero thanked the airman and went around back to get his rucksack. He lugged it to the door and fished in his pocket for his keys. He and Jean had an agreement that if either of them came home when the house lights were off, they would sing out as soon as they got the door open.

He turned on the lights in the hallway just inside the door and said in a loud voice, "The hunter is home from the hill," and shut the door behind him and his rucksack. He saw and heard Jean turn on her bedside light and she came hurriedly to him. She was wearing the short silver satin gown they both liked so much. He thought she was a vision. They hugged for a long time. They both sobbed.

"I am so glad you are home," she said.

"So am I. I missed you so much," he said.

He left his rucksack where it lay by the door and walked with his arm around Jean to the kitchen. She looked him directly in the eyes as they got into the light of the kitchen and kissed him fervently.

When they finally were able to let go of each other, she asked, "Would you like a scrambled egg sandwich?" He grinned and nodded.

As she was scrambling the eggs, he made the toast. He said, "I think I will grab a quick shower. I feel like a man who has slept in his clothes for two nights."

She asked, "Is that because you have slept in your clothes for two nights?"

He nodded.

She said, "Eat your scrambled egg sandwich first, then I will help you wash off that road dust, Road Warrior."

He grinned as he bit into the sandwich.

Somewhere during their reunion, he managed to tell her that he needed to go on to Washington to confer with Mr. Murfree and that he would be leaving the next morning. She rolled over from her position next to him in the bed and landed on top of him.

"You are going to have to wrestle your way out of here, you know," she said with a sly smirk.

"Promises, promises," he said as he wrapped his arms around her.

In the morning, she drove him to Sky Harbor since he needed to go right away and there were no military flights leaving then. He kissed her goodbye and said, "I always want to stay with you and not go." She nodded and patted his arm. Then, he walked with his roll-along bag into the terminal. She watched until he was swallowed up by the crowd.

As he deplaned at Dulles, he grabbed his bag from the carousel and walked into the main concourse. A tall man in a dark suit was holding a card that had printed on it, "Mr. Roman."

He walked up and said, "I am Dan Roman." The driver acknowledged him with a smile and said that the car was at the curb. They walked together out the double metal doors to the sidewalk and to the dark blue Suburban idling at the curb. He opened the door for Lero, who swung his bag into the back seat and got in.

When the drivers dropped him off at the motel, he checked in and went directly to his room. He unwound for a while, then dialed Jean's number.

"Hello," she said.

"How is my favorite roommate?" he asked.

"Well, I hope I am your only roommate," she said with feigned annoyance.

"We had a good flight and I meet with Mr. Murfree tomorrow at ten to report about the latest trip. He asked me to help him here with a situation, so I may need to stay here for a while."

"Oh, phooey," she said. "Doesn't he realize how long you have been away from home?"

"Yes, he does," said Lero. "But he has a serious problem. I need your help with it, too."

"You know that sensor that you and Ernie designed to detect the direction and distance of a cell phone at close range?" he asked.

"Yes, we think it works pretty well, but only if you either know the number of the phone you are sensing or there are only a few phones within the arc of sensitivity that are in operation, so you can narrow down the search," she said. "Do you have a need for it?"

"I think so. What if we used two sensors at ninety degrees from each other, could we sense the position of a cell phone pretty closely?"

"Well, if we used two sensors like that, and they were, say a hundred yards apart, we could locate a cell phone within less than a foot, horizontally."

"What if we used a third sensor set to sense the elevation of the cell phone from the sensor?" he asked.

"With the three sensors working together, we could locate a cell phone within a foot, both horizontally and vertically."

"How long would it take to get three of them packed up and brought with you here?"

"Well, actually, we only have two. I would need to assemble a third one. That would take the better part of a day. I could catch the "red eye" from Sky Harbor late tomorrow night and you could pick me up at Dulles early the next morning."

"What does the sensor look like? How big is one?" he asked.

"A sensor is about the size of a large thirty five millimeter single lens reflex camera," she said.

"If we mounted each of them on a tripod would they look enough like a surveyor's thedolyte to fool most people?" he asked.

"It would not fool an engineer or a surveyor, but a lay person would not know the difference," she said.

"Okay," he said. "Get three together and come east on the red eye. I will meet you at the gate at Dulles."

273

"I can tell by the tension in your voice that this is something important, Dan. I won't ask now, but I hope I can help."

"You and those machines you designed will be a great help. It just gives me a good reason to have you with me here. I love to watch you walk toward me."

"You are sweet to say so, Dan. I will get ready and will call you to confirm my plans."

"Thank you for doing this. It is important."

"I am glad. See you Thursday morning. I love you."

"I love you, too. Good night."

Chapter 69

At Lero's recommendation, Lero and Jean were designated as White House Maintenance Contractors. Each was issued an ID badge with picture and coverall uniforms were provided to identify them further. A memo was sent out to the effect that architectural surveyors would be working around and in the White House for approximately a week. Pictures of Lero and Jean were provided in the memo. So there was not a flutter when Lero and Jean began to set up their scanners. Lero set his up on the north lawn, in plain sight, and Jean put hers up on the east side of the White House, also out in the open. They used cell phones to coordinate.

"If we have the number, we can spot the phone within a foot, but if we don't have the number, we will get so many responses that the result will be meaningless. If I were the sender, I would send my report in the busiest time of the day, to hide in the clutter."

"I had our friends at NSA get us the cell phone numbers of all the people in the White House. The Anti-terrorism office lent us some of their expertise to profile the people and we supplied the profiles. They came up with a list of fourteen suspects. You and I need to sit down with Mr. Murfree and go over this list and see what he thinks," said Lero.

In the morning, they were called for by drivers in a dark brown Denali and made it through traffic from Dulles to downtown D.C. in good time. The Secret Service agent was waiting for them at the gate house and took them and their baggage on a cart into an office on the main floor of the White House.

"The President asked us to give each of you these ID badges. He said you would be working with us for a few days and that your electronic equipment would not interfere with any of our communications devices or sensors. You may use the room down the hall, with the number fourteen on it to stow your gear and as a general headquarters while you are here. Meals are served in the White House cafeteria at regular times. Your ID pass will entitle you to meals, too. Just let us know if we can do anything to help you," he said.

"Thanks, Agent Spaulding. We appreciate the hospitality. We will stay out of your way. This may take a few days."

Lero and Jean went down to room fourteen and stowed their gear. He laid out a map of the White House, a separate sheet for each floor, including all of the basements and the tunnels. They decided where they would place their sensors and he went with her to get hers set up. Since they were battery powered, they did not need any electrical service and could go anywhere they wanted them to. Once she was set up, he left her to go set up his tripod and sensor. Both of them were startled at the number of cell phones in use at any given time in the White House. With the capability of sensing particular phones by number, they were able to begin observing the phones of interest and make notes on their hand held tape recorders. Jean's sensor for horizontal sensing was combined with a vertical sensor. Using their cell phones, they could comment on the placement and movement of each phone as they surveyed them. They soon discovered that, in addition to the cell phones they knew about, there were several trac phones whose numbers they could detect and write down, but whose operators they did not know. Lero was thankful to have the NSA guys recording all of the conversations and texts so they could compare their data with the NSA data to eliminate the callers that were no threat.

Jean's phone buzzed in her pocket. She answered, "Hello." The female voice on the other end asked, "What is the code?"

Jean said "Two six five four."

"The phone with the number ending in 1141 is transmitting coded messages. Word groups and individual words. This is suspicious. Can you tell us where it is just now?"

Jean said, "Let me adjust my sensor. Hold, please," and she put the phone in her pocket, still on. Just as Jean set the number of the phone into the digital pad of the sensor, the screen showed a blip which disappeared immediately."

"They turned off just as I started to scan, but I can tell you that it was in the rear or South side of the White House, but I could not get the vertical sensor on in time to tell which floor."

"Okay," said the voice. "We will alert you if it transmits again."

"Alright," said Jean. "We will continue to survey."

The line went silent. It was the only time that day that the NSA called with an alert. Like most surveillance work, it is long hours of boring observation between exciting moments. Lero and Jean worked all day without another call.

After the second day, they were becoming discouraged with the results. The mysterious cell phone had not become active again, and they only received one alert from the NSA guys all day.

About three o'clock, a messenger brought Lero an envelope. On the card inside was a handwritten message: "Join us for dinner tonight at seven. Janice."

Chapter 70

As they got into their rented car, Lero said "Guess what? Mr. Murfree and Janice invited us to dinner in the residence tonight. Did you bring something appropriate?"

"Not that fancy. I assumed that I would be working mostly and didn't bring anything fancier than my dark blue pants suit.

As they returned to their motel room, Lero drove the rented Grand Cherokee along the bridge toward the Arlington National Cemetery. The road curved to the right and they were once again in heavy traffic. In a couple of miles, he turned the Grand Cherokee into an upscale mall.

"Let's see if they have anything here that would work," he said.

She smiled broadly as she spotted the store names in the mall. What she did not know was that Lero had called ahead to a couturier whose name had been recommended to him, although he knew very little about high fashion. He had told them that he would be arriving at about five PM, and that he would be wearing a red button in his lapel, and that he would be accompanying a lady who did not want to be recognized, but who would require extra attention, who would want to see their collection of designs for an important dinner meeting with foreign dignitaries. As they walked in, a dignified sales lady stepped up and asked, "May I help you?"

Lero said, "Yes, I called earlier, we need something for a dinner meeting."

"Of course," she said. "Does madam have any price range in mind?" she asked.

Lero answered, "No. She is to see the very best you have. I will wait over there," and he pointed with his chin to the lounge area for husbands and other helpless males.

Jean gave him a look of amazement, but instantly recovered and followed the lady to the show area. There were five models already there, wearing a variety of formal dinner wear. Jean was very impressed, but carried it off as if she did this all the time.

Ever the practical one, Jean settled on a very dark wine red dinner dress and a pair of patent leather pumps the same color as the dress.

'Yes," she said, "This will do just fine." She looked over at Lero for his impression and he nodded his approval.

"I will have it wrapped for you, ma'am. You may wait over there with your escort."

"Thank you so much. I appreciate your attention to this for me."

"Oh, not at all. We hope you will come back and that you will tell your confidants about us," she said.

She went over to Lero and said, "Thank you so much. This is such a great treat. I have never had so much attention paid to me or shopped in such a nice store. The lady did not tell me how much the outfit was. She said that she would discuss that with you and that you had made it clear that I could have anything I wanted. She made me feel very special. What a treat. How did you ever find this place?"

Lero grinned like he had been caught with his hand in the cookie jar.

"I asked Mr. Murfree where Janice shops for special occasions."

"This suit is a Versace. It must be very expensive," she said.

"You need something special, Jean, for all you have done and for how sweet you are to me. You can wear this suit for years and remember this trip and how much I love you," he said.

She smiled a sweet smile and said, "I can hardly wait to try it on."

Lero said, "I can hardly wait to watch you."

The sales lady brought the nicely wrapped box to Lero and returned his charge card and thanked them again. Lero thanked her for her attention and carried the box as Jean walked out with him.

"How much did that outfit cost?" she asked under her breath.

He said, "Oh, I forget, but don't worry about it. It is a once in a great while event and I wanted you to be confident that you were properly dressed."

"I'm just a country girl, Dan. All this proximity to the President and the White House sure has an effect, doesn't it?"

"Yes, it does. But Mr. Murfree puts us at ease and Janice is a wonderful hostess. I hope we can solve this problem for them."

He held the door of the Grand Cherokee for her and put the box in the back seat.

Chapter 71

Later, in their room, she opened the box with the glee of a child on Christmas morning. She picked up the dress and held it out to admire it. Then she noticed that the sales lady had included a beautiful dark red slip under the suit and three pairs of designer hose of a nice darker dignified shade. Just when she was about to remark that she could not wear the hose since she had not brought a garter belt, she discovered the dark lace garter belt under the slip, and two pair of high fashion black lace undies. She "ooohed and aaaahd" as she made each new discovery. They took a quick shower to get ready in time for the driver who would pick them up. They took enough time though, to let Lero watch her and help her put on the whole ensemble. He was enthralled again.

Precisely at the appointed time, a black Suburban swept up to the portico at the entry. Lero and Jean stepped out and a man in a blue blazer and khakis got out and opened the door for them.

"Good evening," said the door opener and they returned his greeting. In eight minutes, the Suburban swept up to the south gate of the White House. The driver flashed an ID to the guard and the gate opened smartly.

As the Suburban slowed to a stop at the doorway, President Thompson and the First Lady, Janice, stepped out to greet them. They exchanged pleasantries as they walked to the elevator and soon found themselves on the residence floor. The door to the second room on the right was opened and they stepped into a small dining room. The staff was waiting for them and stood ready to begin serving the meal.

After a silence, President Thompson asked, "Dan, how can we ever repay you for what you have done?"

"Just knowing that we made a positive difference is plenty of satisfaction, sir."

The President turned to the head waiter and asked, "What is on the menu tonight, Martin?"

"Sir, we have a nice tossed salad to lead off, then pan fried trout or oven roasted turkey for entrees. Vegetables are baked potatoes, peas with mushrooms, beets, broccoli, gravy, and dinner rolls. Dessert is peach cobbler with pralines and cream ice cream."

After Martin and the Sous-Chef, Clarisse, served the main course, and withdrew, the President asked Lero how the project was coming along. Janice and Jean stopped mid-conversation to hear his answer.

In a low voice, Lero said, "Well, sir, with the help of our friends at the phone company (NSA), we have discovered the cell numbers of the phones used by the fourteen candidates. Our belief is that he or she is forwarding information as soon after acquisition as possible. Today, speed is paramount with such information. The pros at the phone company said our candidates would be using their cell phones during the middle of the morning, when telephone traffic is the heaviest. Jean and I will be coordinating our efforts using our cell phones while we take positions at ninety degrees apart outside the White House with our scanning devices. The transmissions of information are quite short and we will need to be on our toes to catch the mole. The old days of dead drops and written messages and the like are long passed. Speed is everything now."

"Do you feel secure telling us who the suspects are?" asked the President.

Lero hesitated a moment and said, "We believe that we should withhold that information just now, sir, with your permission. Jean and I have devised a procedure to try to identify the mole and we will be implementing it in the morning. I will alert you as soon as we succeed or fail, if that is alright."

"Sure," said the President. "That is fine. Do you want your peach cobbler with or without the ice cream?"

Jean said to Janice, "Would you tell me where the powder room is, please?"

Janice rose went with Jean to show her where it was. Jean noticed as they left the room, Lero had leaned close to the President and was almost whispering something to him. As they walked toward the ladies room, Jean suddenly stopped, and with her arm, signaled Janice to stand back. Jean put her hand into her purse, went to a door and yanked it open.

Clarisse was so startled by the sudden discovery that she stood for a second or two, wide eyed and paralyzed with inaction, a miniature drill in one hand and a bug in the other. It took only that long for the tranquilizer dart to find her rib cage just below her left breast. She collapsed in a couple of seconds, in a heap, as the diprenorphine (Immobilon) hit her. Jean quickly put the tranquilizer pistol back into her purse and then took pictures of the drill and the bug with her smart phone and Clarisse with the dart stuck in her chest before she summoned the Chief of the Secret Service. Janice recovered from her initial surprise and looked up just as the President and Lero came hurriedly along the hallway. Three Secret Service agents came hustling from the other direction, with guns drawn.

Since they were not "in on" the reason for the activity, the President assured them that it was alright and that Jean and Lero were working for him. He ordered the agent in charge to take Clarisse to a hospital under guard and keep her there under arrest until she could be questioned.

Then, the President, noticing that Lero was hugging Jean and that Jean was a bit shaken up, rounded the four of them up and started them back up the hallway to the residence dining room.

When they got there, the President asked Jean how he knew Clarisse was the mole.

"Well, sir, we had narrowed the list to three. Ernie had just texted me on my cell phone that she was the prime suspect, identifying her by number, so I wore my ear mike. He contacted me through it and said that she was transmitting nearby, so I asked to go the ladies room and, using my hand held sensor, located her in the cloak room in the hallway. I knew from our blueprints that the back wall of the cloak room backs up to the back wall of your private study. It looked to me like she was about to install a bug in that wall, so I immobilized her. I hope I did not startle you, Janice."

"Oh, no," smirked Janice. "We have shootouts most evenings during dessert."

They all shared a laugh.

After they enjoyed their peach cobbler, President Thompson and Janice walked Lero and Jean back to the south portico, President Thompson said, "I know you need to stop by the Secret Service Office and give statements, but once you get back to Tucson and get your team recovered and the details taken care of, Janice and I want you to spend a week, just the two of you, at our place in Vail. We will coordinate with you after you return to Tucson, so we can agree on a time. Our G-Five (Gulfstream Five corporate jet) is going to Honolulu tomorrow morning to pick up the Vice President and his family. Why don't you let me have them drop you off in Tucson on the way?"

"That is very generous, sir. Thank you. We will be ready."

"I will have a driver pick you up. They will call with a time. Thank you both again, so much, for what you have done. It is a great comfort to Janice and me to know that you are there for us. Have a safe trip. See you soon."

Handshakes and hugs were exchanged at the door. The four had become good friends in the two years that Lero and Jean had worked for Unit Forty Seven.

Jean laid her head on Lero's shoulder as the Suburban whisked them out of the White House grounds.